Verbosity
Constrained

Steve Recchia

ISBN:978-1-7357224-0-5

DEDICATION

This is dedicated to a censor who has requested anonymity. See F-Bomb Alert, Only the Names Have Been Changed, The Interview After the Sermon, and Legalize Sanity.

Verbosity Constrained

MALCONTENTS

Verbosity Constrained

CONSTRAINTS

How many words does it take to tell a story? There's a legend that Ernest Hemingway won a bet by writing a story six words in length. The San Luis Obispo *New Times* has an annual short fiction contest, 55Fiction, in which each story has at most 55 words, and, in addition, at most 7 more words for a title. There are a number of other opportunities to publish and read very short fiction, each with its own particular constraints, usually much more than just 55 words. Sometimes, however, it's best to just step out of the way and let the story tell itself, no matter how many words it wants. There are also times when the constraints may involve rhythms and rhymes, subject matter, or style, rather than length.

One of the greatest joys of my young life was making my mother laugh about things that she obviously did not feel she should be laughing about. Some of these stories, poems, and letters may have a similar effect on the reader. Some of them may provide more of a thought provoking jolt. Constraints can also involve attitudes and beliefs. Anyone who feels there should be constraints on questions regarding authority or convention might do well to stop right here.

The words and illustrations here are mine. Any close resemblance to anything done previously by others is unintentional. Any close resemblance to actual persons and events is unavoidable, and, in some cases, intentional.

Steve Recchia
verbosity_constrained@gmail.com
September, 2020

Verbosity Constrained

GOTTA START SOMEPLACE

The First Argument

"Here. Have just a little taste."
"No, thanks."
"This fruit is the best!"
"I'm not hungry right now."
"Just try one bite."
"I don't want any."
"How come it's always about what you want? How come it's never about what I want?"
"We're not supposed to..."
"Just take one bite! Who's ever gonna know, Adam?"

Really? That's It?

"I've got to say that I'm impressed with your experience, your recommendations, and with everything we've discussed so far. But it would be dishonest of me if I didn't tell you that you'll face massive amounts of stress and frustration if you accept this job. Some of the people you'll have to interact with most often, quite frankly, will be uncooperative, unreliable, disrespectful, and even hostile at times. Do you think you're equipped to deal with that?"
"I've been married for twenty years and I've got three teenagers at home."
"How soon can you start?"

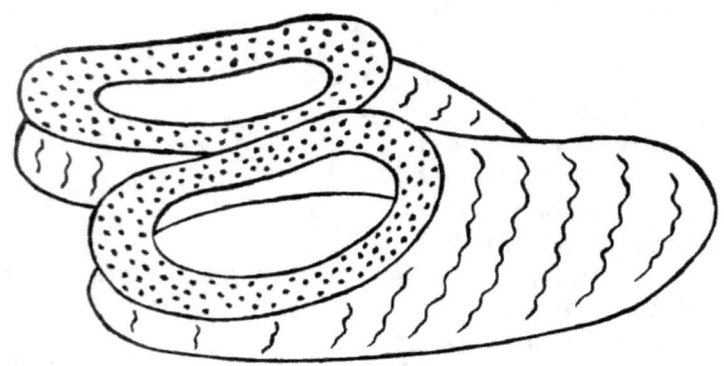

Bathrobe Pending

"You're really into this new guy."
"Yeah."
"He treating you well?"
"Yeah."
"Is he working?"
"Yeah."
"Using drugs?"
"No."
"Drinking?"
"A little."
"Sleeping together?"
"Some."
"Leaving stuff at his place?"
"Toothbrush and slippers for now. Bathrobe next week. Why all the questions?"
"You've made some bad choices in the past. I worry about you, Mom."

It's the Thought That Counts

"It's great you could make it for lunch! We haven't
gotten together for months. What's new?"
"I decided to make some major lifestyle changes."
"Since when?"
"Last couple months. So far, it's working out fine."
"Like what?"
"A vegan diet, for starters."
"But you just ordered a cheeseburger."
"So far, I'm only vegan between meals."

The Maneuver

"How was your date last night?"
"OK, until she stopped breathing."
"Stopped breathing?!?!"
"A piece of bread got stuck in her airway. I finally got
behind her and squeezed her abdomen hard."
"Strange!"
"That's nothing...She says she's never been so
aroused before and wants to do it again."
"You can sure pick 'em, Heimlich."

The End of Time

"Are you still up?"
"This is so cool! I just made the best universe ever! I randomized the initiation parameters and started with a big explosion! There are galaxies, and stars, and planets, and..."
"That's nice, Honey, but..."
"Life evolved! Carbon-based life! That's never happened before! Never! I have to analyze all the parameters!"
"Not tonight. I'm turning this thing off right now."
"No! It's not backed up yet! I don't even know the parameters! I'll lose everything!"
"Maybe you'll listen next time I tell you to go to bed. It's a school night."

The New Partner

"Nice little operation you've got here, real potential, but cash flow is a problem. My godfather is your new partner. We'll franchise, move headquarters to Rome. One more thing... If you don't pay for the wine, fish, and bread by next week, either you're on the cross, or your mother's face won't look so good."

Now It Makes Sense That We Don't

"As Chairman, I want to thank each of you for your hard work. This is our best universe yet, stunning and beautiful beyond words. Now it's time to lighten up a bit. We still need a dominant species for one last world. Have fun. Go crazy with this one. Throw logic totally out the window."

Just a Little Nudge

"Happy 50th anniversary! Four children, twelve grandchildren, nine great grandchildren! How did Grandpa ask you to marry him?"
"He didn't, but I didn't know that for the first ten years. After we dated for three years, your great grandmother bribed our Chinese waiter. We both got fortune cookies that said 'Will you marry me?'"

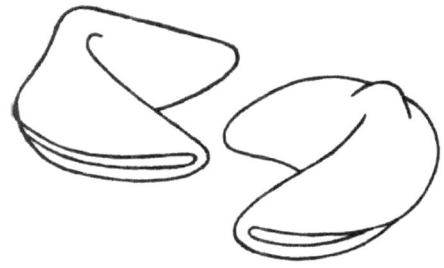

I Wouldn't Have Missed It

"Congratulations! You're such a beautiful bride!"
"Thanks. I'm so glad you could come!"
"I wouldn't have missed it for the world. How long have you two known each other?"
"Three years, but we both knew we'd be together the minute we met! What do you think?"
"I think that he'll make a wonderful first husband."

Yeah, Really

Many times I haven't changed in ways that I should.
Now it seems a bit of change might do me some good.
I'll start being nice and stop being such a grouch.
Stop watching TV so much, sitting on the couch.
I'll get back to working out, and I'll lose 10 pounds.
I'll get into shape again, love the way that sounds.
I'm done with the unhealthy dietary trash.
I'll stop wasting money, and save more of my cash.
You chuckle, skeptical. This time I'm not joking.
I'll be chewing celery. Yeah, I'm quitting smoking.
Decrease my carbon footprint, and bike or else walk.
Composting and recycling, I'll do more than talk.
I'll do a lot more reading, stimulate my brain.
I'll fix that leaky faucet, clean out that slow drain.
There won't be a limit to all the things I'll do.
Clean the basement, the garage, clean the attic, too.
Clean out all the closets, and toss out those old pants.
I'll be reconnecting and write to all my aunts.
I'll start remembering birthdays, holidays, and such.
I'll be sending cards and notes to say thanks so much.
When someone's rude or pushy, or gets in my way,
I'll be patient, smile, and hope they have a nice day.
When I'm out in traffic, unto others, I'll do.
My new favorite mantra will now be "After you."
Show consideration, give benefit of doubt.
I'll count to ten more often. There's no need to shout.
I'll clean up my language, quit dropping the f-bomb.
You'll be wanting me to meet your dad and your mom.
No more viewing life with hostile apprehension.
I'll even cut back middle finger extension.
Seeing all these changes, your jaw may hit the floor.
You might even wonder if I'm me anymore.
I've mostly tried my best, too often done my worst.
Now I'm optimistic. It's January 1st.

DAILY APPLES NOTWITHSTANDING

Who's Your First Choice?

"Donnie Corleone here, for The Organization. We've diversified into healthcare. We're more profitable than ever, and still committed to the same family ethics as always. We've evolved since my great grandfather's day. Why bother with beatings and cement shoes when we've got ICU's, nursing homes, and insurance? We'll make you an offer you can't refuse!"

Healthcare Update

"Honey, look at this! It says I just had an expiration date reset! My new expiration date is in three weeks! There must be some mistake!"
"What?"
"It says I'm not cost effective anymore because even with all the medications, my blood pressure and diabetes aren't controlled. My projected maintenance costs exceed my productivity by 30%. Look at this!"
"Let's see. You're entitled to medication for relaxation. And to a Class 1 termination party! Those are good! Excellent catering and drinks, incredible bands... Towards the end of the evening, you'll just go to sleep, and..."
"I'm only 37!"
"It says here if you don't cooperate, you'll have a Class 4 termination during halftime at The Game of the Week. Those are rough! And we haven't been to a good party for a long time. Here, Sweetie, have a drink."

The Current State of the Chess Set

"This chess set is unusual. The pieces are in business suits, hospital gowns, and white coats."
"The Healthcare Set. The larger pieces, the suits, are executives, politicians, accountants. The smaller pieces, in the gowns and white coats, are patients and physicians. They're the pawns."
"How much is it?"
"That depends. Call this 800 number."

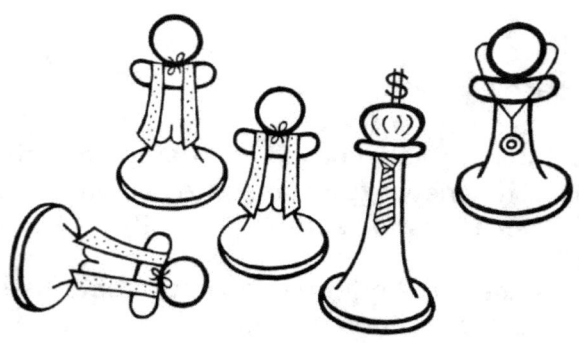

You Look Inside Me

"I've never told you this before, but I appreciate you so much more than words alone could ever say. You care! You're the only woman in the whole world who actually pays attention when I open my mouth. You really want me to open my mouth."
"Of course I do! I'm your dentist! Now open!"

Behavior Modification

"There's no question about your diagnosis: carpal tunnel syndrome."
"Will I need surgery?"
"Possibly, but since this is generally due to repetitive motion, changing your activity may be enough."
"What should I do?"
"Stop patting yourself on the back so much."

Rude Awakening

"Wake up! Give me all your money or you're dead!"
"What? Wait a minute... You just broke in?"
"You heard me! The money! Now!"
"Thank you. I do appreciate this."
"What?"
"They've recommended surgery, then chemotherapy. That may give me a little more time. Maybe... This'll be better. Can I make you some coffee first?"

In One Ear

"Your father is brain dead. His heart, lungs, liver and kidneys have all failed. The infection is overwhelming."
"But..."
"There's no chance your father will survive. It's time to withdraw support."
"Doc, you've said all that before. But Katie's getting married next week. He doesn't want to miss that. When can we take him home?"

The Network Before the Horse

"Are you in my insurance network?"
"I don't know. I'm in lots of them."
"Then get out of here! I can afford to die, but I can't afford out-of-network medical bills."
"I'm the only physician here. Your insurance should cover emergency treatment. You're having a heart attack. Are you still having chest pain?"
"Not since they put that medicine under my tongue."
"What were you doing when it started?"
"Watching the presidential debate. Some idiot was talking about having medical coverage for everybody. I got so mad I... Uh! My... chest! It's... bad!"

Roses, Sunsets, and Deadlines

"My life had become a series of sprints from one deadline to the next, with little time for smelling roses or watching sunsets. That's all changed. Now I'm enjoying roses, and sunsets are very special to me, despite a major impending deadline."
"That's wonderful! We may be able to extend that deadline with more chemotherapy."

In the Wool

"Four weeks ago you couldn't move your left side. Now you're walking again. These medications will decrease the risk of another stroke."
"I might need to have another stroke."
"Why?!?! You could become totally disabled!"
"Because now I lean to the left when I walk. I'm a conservative. I want to lean to the right."

Navigating the System

"You've heard from our guests, each of them abducted by aliens. The phone lines are open. Here's our first caller."
"Hello. What do they charge? Is referral required?"
"You've reached Alien Abduction Debriefing. This is a talk show."
"Right. They've all had the rectal probe."
"Sir, what…"
"I'm changing insurance. I'm overdue for a colonoscopy."

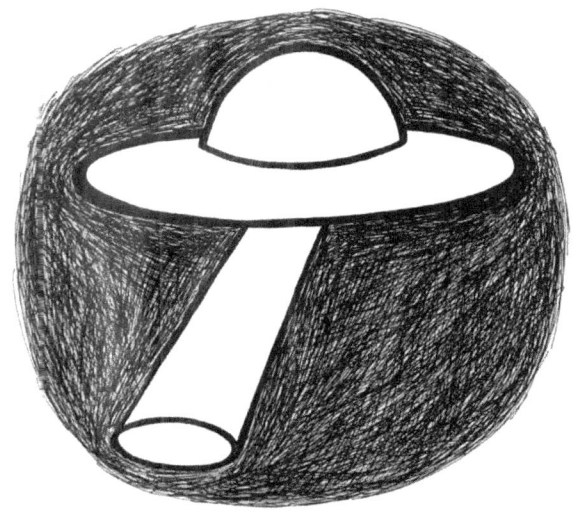

HOME FOR THE HOLIDAYS

What's Not for Dinner?

To: Extended Family

From: The Pseudo Perfect Couple

Re: Holiday Dinner

See you all at five for our annual family holiday dinner. We'll provide all the appetizers, salads, entrees, side dishes, bread, desserts, coffee, wine, and soft drinks. We'd like everyone else to please bring enough tolerance to serve about 20. We'll be prepared to clean up any accidental spillage of red wine or gravy. However, any spillage of politics into this diverse group may be much more difficult and awkward to clean up. Please leave yours at home this time. Thanks! See you then!

Part of the Family

"Thanks for inviting my whole family for Thanksgiving dinner!"
 "I've offered to have holiday dinners the last couple years, but they've refused."
 "They finally accept you as part of the family."
"Next year I'll show them I really am part of the family."
"By inviting them again?"
"By getting out of it, like everyone else."

One Set of Instructions

"The only time we ever get together with them anymore is for holidays. All I'm saying is don't bring up anything provocative."
"I'll never understand how anyone with that much education could be so…"
"Stop! Don't discuss the weather."
"The weather? Why not?"
"Climate change. And no talk of hunting or deer tags."
"Why not?"
"Gun control. And nothing about anyone's health or healthcare."
"So what can I talk about?"
"Gardening, seeing the kids and grandkids, getting the whole family together. Those should be safe topics."
"This is crazy! I'm taking a bottle of whiskey."

Another Set of Instructions

"We only see them for the holidays. Just don't start anything."
"Me? I don't get how anyone who ran a business for that many years could be so…"
"Don't! Make sure you don't mention gardening."
"Gardening? But…"
"They've got peach trees, only one step away from impeachment. And no talk of kids or grandkids."
"That's ridiculous!"
"Reproductive rights. And nothing about getting the whole family together."
"But that's…"
"Kids in cages. Talk about the weather, or your hunting trip, or how good your health has been."
"This is stupid. I'm taking a bottle of whiskey."

Finally, Common Ground?

"Good to see you. It's been, what, about a year?"
"Yeah. How've you been?"
"I'm, uh, not supposed to talk about that. Or the weather, or..."
"The weather?"
"But gardening, the kids, the grandkids, and getting the whole family together should all be OK."
"I'm not supposed to talk about any of those. This is stupid! But I brought a bottle of whiskey."
"Wonderful! Me, too! Some twenty year-old Kentucky..."
"Kentucky?!?! This stuff from Tennessee is way better! Anyway, let's have some."
"OK. I'll get some glasses and ice."
"Ice? Ice! Are you serious?"

There's No Place Like Home

"Monsters under the bed?"
"Keep in mind, last night was the first time I've slept in
this house, in that bed, in thirty years."
"What'd they look like? Powerful jaws? Giant claws?"
"Like I never would've expected! Like the kids down
the street, their parents, a couple teachers, a scout
leader..."

The Word Shortage Has Officially Ended

"You survived a three-day weekend with my
family! You even met Uncle Wally, and talked with him
for an hour without trying to escape!"
"He's quite the talker! You could've warned me!"
"You didn't need any warning. You can out-Wally
Wally any day of the week. Maybe I should've warned
him!"

Parental Encouragement

"It's been a great visit, but I shouldn't have stayed for
a whole week. I forgot how stressful some of the
interactions can be in this family. I mean, I love
Grandma and Uncle..."
"That's exactly why you need to get married and start
your own family. Then this one won't seem quite so
bad."

GETTING SOME OF IT ALL TOGETHER

An Introspective Moment

"There's no need to be so crude. It says here that the sculptor captured a quiet moment of introspection."
"It's a guy with his head up his ass. What's the title?"
"Administrative Yoga."

How Should I Start?

"It's been tough lately, with loved ones sick and dying, job loss, bankruptcy, eviction, insomnia…. I've heard meditation might help. How should I start?"
"Try to relax and focus on your breathing. When other thoughts intrude, try to return your focus to your breathing. It'll be hard. You have a lot to not think about."

Focus

Inhale... pick up some avocados... gently... and a lime... slowly... cilantro... almonds... chest rising... sugar snaps... oil change can wait until tomorrow... deeply... oops, hope nobody smells that... gently... that old hermit down the road could use a meal... focus... that new shop by the tracks... focus... did a good job last time... the air moving in... the woman in purple got a new haircut... cherry tomatoes... and out... only two weeks for this new project... focus... get real... gently... it's warm in here today... focus... some of those crisp rye crackers... chest falling... two weeks, no way... focus... the basil needs watering... gently... today... focus...forgot to do the laundry... on breathing... some young, tender carrots... let it all out... I'd better go in early for the next... relax... couple weeks... focus... dammit!

Mindfulness

"Thanks for coming. I hope you enjoyed the weekend retreat."
"More than I could ever tell you! The meditation and yoga sessions were so satisfying! Maintaining silence for the whole weekend seemed awkward at first, but the mindfulness was unbelievable! I'm aware of every breath and every heartbeat. I'm even aware of my feet!"
"Namaste."

Mindfulness, Influenced

"Great party, dude! Thanks."
"Are you OK to drive? You had several of the Bourbon barrel aged stouts."
"That stuff is incredible! Especially the ones from Michigan, Missouri, and California. Don't worry, I'm OK to drive. I'm hyper alert. I'm even aware of my feet!"
"Your feet, huh? I'm definitely calling a cab for you."

Mindfulness, Cut Short

"How are you today?"
"I'm better today, Doc. The pain control is OK. I ate a little. I still haven't been up."
"Good. Do you remember being out on patrol last week, Sergeant?"
"Vaguely... Hey, I'm even aware of my feet!"
"Uh, yeah... Listen, you, uh, don't actually have feet anymore."

Mindfulness, Facilitated

"What a hike! It was beautiful!"
"Yeah! Being on top of the mountain at sunset, watching the full moon rise at the same time, and then hiking out by moonlight."
"That mountain has a great memory. I'd forgotten how old my hips and knees are. It reminded me. And I'm intensely aware of my feet."

And Breathe

"How was the week-long meditation and yoga retreat? Was it everything you'd hoped it would be?"
"No description could ever do it justice! The intensity of the focus required, and the resulting relaxation, both surpassed, by far, anything I'd ever experienced before. I feel I've switched to an entirely new path, and taken the first steps on a long, amazing, rewarding journey. Now I've got the tools I need for all that lies ahead. I can't possibly thank you enough. Your suggestion that I attend the retreat, and your generosity in paying for my registration, was the best gift you could have ever given me. Thank you!"
"You're welcome. You know that I would do anything for you. What's next?"
"I've got to simplify, to eliminate all the unnecessary clutter from my life. I'll be moving out tomorrow."

PICKLES

Her Perspective

"He's perfect! I'll take him. Thanks, you're a lifesaver."

"You're welcome. He looks just like all the others, all black except for the small white patch on his chest, and with the same greenish-gold eyes. I think he's the fifth identical cat I've gotten for you in the last, what, fifteen years?"

"Eighteen years. We always send my mother the same family photo every year. All of us on the sofa, a year older, with Pickles on my lap. We wouldn't want Mom to think anything happened to Pickles. She probably thinks he's the oldest cat in the world."

"Your mother must be very attached to him."

"Actually, they've never met. Mom thinks we have so much cat fur around the house that we could bale it. She never comes to visit because she's allergic to cats."

And Her Perspective

"Isn't that sweet! Eighteen photos on your wall of your daughter, her family, and their cat, one every year. Such a lovely tradition!"
"She's very thoughtful."
"They're always on the sofa in the same order, with the cat on her lap. That cat must be getting old."
"It's a charming image. If you look very closely, you can see they're actually on about their fifth cat now. I'm supposed to think it's the same one, that it's getting old, and that they're terribly attached to him."
"Do you visit them often?"
"Never. But my daughter understands, because of my severe allergy to cats."
"You're not allergic to cats."
"Don't tell my daughter."

Yet Another Perspective

"This is so cool! I love it that you wrote these stories about me, my mom, and Pickles. And then published them in a book, with an illustration, no less! My sister will love them, too. I can't wait to share them with her."
"I was hoping you'd enjoy them. The stories just kind of showed up after you told me about your mom and your cat. So I wrote them down, with a little artistic license, of course. I also thought that including these stories in the collection might triple the book sales."
"Triple the sales? Really? Why?"
"Instead of just my mom buying a copy, I thought you'd probably buy a copy for yourself, and one for your sister, too."
"Wait, you mean I can't just take a picture of those pages with my phone? Oh, uh, say, listen, I'm, uh, kind of late. Gotta go! See you later!"

PRINCE CHARMING ENOUGH

The Perfect Man

"Isaac yelled."
"Kenny smelled."
"Nathan snored."
"Ollie ignored."
"Wally smoked."
"Harry croaked."
"Everett hit."
"Stanley spit."
"Orion's lewd."
"Uriah's rude."
"Tom leeched."
"Tim preached."
"Hunter blabbed."
"Ender grabbed."
"Richard strayed."
"Evan played."
"Sherman lied."
"Otto cried."
"Manny whined."
"Ezra pined."
"Peter peeked."
"Larry reeked."
"Alex couldn't."
"Charlie wouldn't."
"Ethan shouldn't."
"Waiter! More wine!"

A Good Sponsor Is Hard to Find

"My name is Princess. I'm addicted to online dating."
"Hi, Princess."
"I've been dating from three different websites, 25 guys every month. I want my life back. I've never been in a 12-step program before. I'll need a sponsor, someone caring and communicative, 45 - 55 years old, a guy who likes the beach."

Why Waste Time?

"Thanks to all of you for taking the Paradise Senior Living tour today. If you have any questions..."
"My wife just passed. Could I try one of your apartments tonight?"
"We might be able to arrange that."
"My husband left this world last week. Could I share that same apartment tonight?"

There's Something We Need to Discuss

"Yes, I'd love to marry you, but..."
"But, what?"
"I look like a woman, I feel like a woman, I am a woman, but I was born a male. I still have my..."
"Wonderful! Do you want children?"
"You don't under..."
"I understand perfectly. I look like a man, I feel like a man, but. ."

A Very Special Guy

"A wedding? No way! I've got a game this afternoon."

"Not anymore you don't. You're the father of the bride. Jenny's getting married today!"

"What?!?! I'm just hearing about this now?"

"I just heard about it myself."

"I didn't even know she had a boyfriend."

"Just listen. I'll tell you what she just told me. You remember Ray? He grew up next door?"

"Yeah, sure. He's a good guy. He's the one?"

"He's the one."

"Well, they've known each other for their whole lives, so he ought to know what he's getting into. Her sense of humor and her practical jokes are going to require a very special guy."

"No kidding! I still remember the exploding birthday cake."

"Who could forget that one? And how about the booby-trapped toilet seat, with the 5 AM blast of cold water?"

"I'm glad that was your butt instead of mine. Anyway, Ray was going to get married today. His future in-laws met Ray for the first time about an hour ago, at Ray's place. Jenny said she just happened to be there. The fiancé's father is a minister who walked in, looked at the TV, looked at Ray, and started screaming things you might not expect to hear from a minister. Then they left. The wedding is off. At least, that one is. Remember, Jenny was there the whole time. She got it all on video. Afterwards, she and Ray laughed a lot, and decided they'd get married today. All the arrangements have already been made."

"I'll be damned! I can't wait to shake his hand!"

"That may be difficult. Ever since about one minute before his fiancé and her parents arrived, Ray has had a TV remote superglued to his right hand, and the case for a porno DVD superglued to his left."

Investigations in Flux

"Can I come in?"

"Sure, unless you'd rather stand in the doorway all afternoon. How can I help you?"

"We'll get to that in a minute. Am I a tall, cool drink on a hot summer day?"

"What the…"

"Is there anything in your filing cabinet other than three drawers of California climate and what's left in the office bottle?"

"Who the…"

"And when is the last time you actually did an investigation? Other than trying to find a clean pair of socks?"

"Did you come here just to lift my spirits? Or is there some point…"

"OK. I'll start at the beginning. My husband disappeared about six weeks ago. At first, I had all the usual worries. Who was she? How could I have been such a fool?"

"It happens."

"Just listen, OK? I went to another private investigator. He took the case. Then, nothing. Absolutely nothing!"

"It takes time develop leads."

"When I say nothing, I mean nothing! No trace of my husband. No trace of the investigator. And now, no trace of any other private investigator! You're it! You're the only one left! And you can't even remember the last time you had a case. Don't you get it?"

"Get what?"

"Do I have to explain everything to you?"

"Maybe you could try telling me something that makes sense."

"Is there anything left in the office bottle?"

"You're putting me through all of this so you can hit me up for a glass of cheap whiskey? Lady, you're crazy."

"Just pour it. Yeah. And listen. God, this stuff is awful! Aged in oak for, what? Twenty minutes? I don't care. Drink up, because you're gonna need it."

"OK, Sweetheart, get to the point."

"I've thought this through. Here's the only thing that makes any sense. Mysteries aren't selling so well these days. We're characters created by one of the last surviving mystery authors, and our days are numbered. We can't even be sure we're going to make it to the next page!"

"As I said earlier, you're crazy!"

"OK, I'll prove it to you. That's your car outside, right? Ten years old, nondescript, great for surveillance, right?"

"Well, yeah. So what?"

"And look at you. You're, what? Sixty? Pretty thin on top, but not so in the middle. And below the paunch, maybe things don't work like they used to. Or as often."

"If you just came here to bust my..."

"I came here to save us."

"There is no us."

"There won't be if you don't get on board pretty quick. Shut up and kiss me!"

"But, I... mmm... mmm... mmm..."

"Just a minute. Take another sip of this whiskey. Yeah, see what I mean? It's getting better. Let's get your jacket off. And loosen the tie. Now, where were we? Mmm... mmm..."

"You may be crazy, but you're very persuasive."

"OK, so look out the window at your car."

"It's... it's gone! And somebody parked their car where mine was!"

"You still don't get it, do you? That's your new car. But we've got to do a lot better than this, or we're history."

"I'm actually starting to believe you! OK, so if mysteries are out, then, what? Action! Come on! Let's get in my new car right now! It'll be great in chase scenes!"

"And you think I'm crazy! First, I don't want anybody shooting at me. Second, you'd probably kill us in a rollover. Third, that kind of action doesn't sell as well as you think. And, most importantly, our author isn't into that kind of action."

"How would you know what kind of action our alleged author isn't into?"

"Because you're still sixty and paunchy. But the car is way better. And so's the whiskey. Roll your sleeves up!"

"Oh, I get it! Another kind of action! Yeah! I'll be the pizza delivery guy, and you'll be the lonely housewife! Oh, yeah!"

"Somehow, I don't think that's it. Think! Or we won't make it to the next page! We kissed, then your car and the whiskey both got a lot better. We're on the right track. Hold me! Kiss me! Tenderly... yes, like that... yes... yes."

"Oh, yeah. I could spend eternity in your arms!"

"You're catching on! Good! Just a minute. Yes! You look a little younger now! More hair! Less paunch! Look out the window! At your car!"

"I'll be damned!"

"Kiss me again! Tell me you love me!"

"I'll always love you! Always!"

"You have a full head of wavy hair! No paunch! And rippling muscles under a golden tan! Oh, darling!"

"I'll see you in the next chapter!"

Proofreading

"Who did the proofreading for you?"

"The women who love me. Nobody notices my mistakes the way they do."

ON THE HEELS OF HEMINGWAY'S SHOES

Deity available. Weddings. Funerals. Reasonable.

For sale. Mommy's fifth wedding ring.

"Be careful where you point that..."

Estate sale. Anger. Hatred. Ignorance. Expensive.

Respectful listener available. Inquire in mirror.

That's disgusting! How much is it?

Support group. Mondays. Other people suck.

They prayed to God. Satan answered.

Assassin available. Politics. Business. Religion.
Love.

We purchased a supply of optimism.

The tombstone says "Finally Quit Drinking."

Futility beckoned. The competition was fierce.

Identity Theft Crime Report. Name: God.

The vows didn't specifically prohibit hatred.

Pandemic preparation ignored. Death went viral.

Walmart
butcher knife
carpet
shovel
cleanser

AS THYSELF

On the Playa

"Hi, neighbors! I must have been asleep when you came in overnight. We usually have the whole playa to ourselves this time of year, just us in our Winnebago. That's quite a rig you've got there. You guys must be Burners. You're a couple months early. Burning Man's not until August. Where are you fellas from?"

"We're researchers from Central Galactic University, here to collect specimens."

"Uh, huh. Well, nice to meet you. I hear the missus waking up... Gotta go... Honey, there's a couple of Burners out here. Their rig looks like a spaceship."

Something to Look Forward To

"You stop that right now! How many times have I told you not to do that?!?! And you keep doing it! Why do you keep doing that?"

"Well, uh, I was talking with the old guy across the street the other day. He said this might be risky to mention, that it'd probably just make things worse, but that it might work."

"What?"

"I'm only thirteen now, so compared to the things I'll be doing that'll make you mad in a few years, maybe this isn't so bad."

"He's probably right. But you're still grounded."

Learning the Basics

"Hi! Is this enough snow for you?"
"More than enough, and it's still coming down. I'll be shoveling forever."
"Have you seen my son?"
"He went that way, with a snow shovel in his hand. He said he wanted to earn some extra cash."
"He always does that as soon as the first flake falls. He was supposed to be home by four."
"Well, now he'll be learning something that's extremely important in life."
"Learning to work is important, sure. But learning to listen is important. Learning to do what he's told is important."
"I didn't mean learning to work. He can learn to work any time. He may even learn to listen and to do as he's told someday. Maybe. But if he's ever going to marry, he'll definitely have to learn how to make excuses."

Clerical Error

"It looks like that house across the street from you finally sold."
"Yeah. It's now a halfway house for registered sex offenders."
"Oh! I guess that explains all those clergymen I've seen coming and going. It's really good that they come so often to support fallen members of their congregations."
"Those clergymen all live there."

O, Ye of Little Faith

"I didn't think I'd finish this."
"O, ye of little faith."
"I'd never written so quickly."
"O, ye of scribbled haste."
"It had to be completely reorganized."
"O, ye of cut and paste."
"You promised you wouldn't do this!"
"O, me of switch and bait."
"I'm so annoyed I could spit!"
"O, ye of spittle hate."
"Argh! Sizzled wraith! Vittle place! Livid face!
Fizzled date, nibbled taste, dribbled baste! Riddles
chaste, piddled gate, civil mate, devil raced, deadline
late, twiddled wait, kibble waste! Is that enough?
You're driving me crazy!"
"O, ye of jacket straight."

The Neighbors from Hell

"You've got new neighbors again? Any better than
the last ones?"
"Even worse. Inconsiderate liars! Coming and going
at all hours, parties, noise, booze, babes, sleaze.
Each new one says he'll clean up the last one's mess,
then makes it worse."
"I told you 30 years ago not to buy next to the
governor's mansion."

Love Without Sin

"Come in! What a surprise! Honey! Look who's here!"

"Well, well! What brings you here?"

"No visit to my parents would be complete without a visit next door to my second parents. How have you been?"

"Fine. We both retired."

"Congratulations! What have you been up to?"

"I'm writing a book."

"Really! About what?"

"It's called 'Love Without Sin.' A man's wife is in the ICU, and..."

"I'm so sick of that damned book!"

"...so he spends a lot of time in the waiting room, where he meets a woman whose husband is also..."

"He wouldn't have called it 'Love Without Sin' if he could still..."

"Well, she wouldn't have died in the ICU if she hadn't been smoking for 50 years!"

"Oh, yeah? Well, he wouldn't..."

"Ah, listen, I'm late for dinner with my parents. It was great seeing you! Gotta go! Bye!"

Late Nights and Early Mornings

"Are your neighbors still having loud parties until 3 AM?"

"That may be changing. Lately, whenever anyone in the neighborhood gets rid of old clothes and furniture, my troublesome neighbors have a **7 AM** garage sale. About 50 people show up between 7 and 9. Come by **tomorrow** morning."

"I'm really surprised!"

"So are they."

DUBYA LOOKS BETTER THESE DAYS

Vlad the Bad

My name is Vlad the Bad, and I own Lapdog Don.
Nothing for the vet to cut, he's not got them on.
You wonder what I've got, on a dude that's so rich.
I've got enough dirt that Don the Con is my bitch.
Got bunches of stuff he doesn't want to get out.
Yeah, the devil's in the details, and that's my clout.
They ask me "Got a pee tape in your video hoard?"
If that's all I've got you'd be way too bored.
Well, of course, we filmed it every time that he came,
But all of the sex was never more than a game.
You don't even care that I stole your election.
Your minds are engrossed with this pervert's
      erection.
The sex was just one of so many distractions,
A smoke screen for shady financial transactions.
See, the business deals, no way I'm gonna play nice.
He'd better behave, I've got his nuts in a vice.
I've got proof of his deeds, the evidence lingers.
He's my Yes Man, with every snap of my fingers.
The attorneys are eager to count up the beans,
And now everyone knows what emoluments means.
If you find out too much, that's when this sucker
      burns,
Gets it up the wazoo, if you see his returns.
I took the Crimea, and you know that's a fact.
But you're not watching me, you're watching this
      clown's act.
Yeah, Syria's cool, I'd like it all for my own.
The Embarrassment-in-Chief pulled out of my zone.
Any tune I may call, however crazy, he'll dance.
And he'll do it right now, no heads up in advance.
Constant lies, distortions, and alternative facts,
Disrupting multinational defensive pacts.
Despite numerous witnesses, some just won't see,
This narcissistic sociopath works for me.

He can't commit treason, his own party will say.
They'll accept anything, as long as they can still play.
Have you had enough yet of this Loser-in-Chief?
You're just starting to grasp the whole concept of
    grief.
You think it can't get worse, too much American
    strife?
You best get used to it fools. I'll make him leader for
    life.

December, 2018

F-BOMB ALERT!

Please be advised that there is an embedded f-bomb dropped in the following poem. A very affordable panel of preliminary readers has opined that the political, sexual, and religious content contained in this collection might otherwise not be sufficiently edgy, and has recommended such inclusion.

Multimodal Swamp Management

A frequently bankrupt reality show ham
Hatched a plan to pull off a bigger, better scam.

Tried to look legitimate, maximized the pomp,
Started making claims he was gonna drain a swamp.

It was as true as anything else he's ever said.
This would be his best chance to really knock 'em
    dead.

Milk that swamp for all it's worth, grab all that he can.
Devise and implement an autocratic plan.

First of all, suckers must believe he's filthy rich.
After six bankruptcies, he'd have to have a pitch.

See, this would necessitate yet another loan,
Not an easy sell when your reputation's blown.

Normally, this takes a lot more wealth than bluster.
Collateral. Their own mom? They'd never trust 'er.

Banks originating loans want their money back.
Otherwise, loan officers tend to get the sack.

Enter Deutsche Bank, the money laundering pros.
With the proper backing, they'd no qualms such as
    those.

Tag, VTB, the Russian state-owned bank, was it.
Underwrite the con man's loans? Oh, yeah! Every
    bit.

Unethical? So some suspicious skeptics think,
But there's absolutely nothing wrong here! Wink,
    wink.

VTB salivates. Return on investment?
How about control of a spineless president?

Just a sec. How'd this guy ever get elected?
Wikileaks? And Facebook ads that weren't rejected?

Russian cash and influence, via NRA?
How about Ms. Butina getting put away?

Was that interference? Don't trust the NSA,
DIA, FBI, for sure not CIA.

Ensure your party won't hold you accountable.
They'll build obstacles that are insurmountable

For troublesome watchdogs pushing legal action,
Thereby preventing investigatory traction.

An investigation? Kick someone out the door.
US Attorney? Recall an ambassador?

Inspectors General? Intelligence expert?
Find another lackey to cover up the dirt.

Gag them with an NDA. Call it classified.
Appeal the subpoenas. Claim witnesses all lied.

Redact all passages that may incriminate.
Make sure that all your staffers keep their stories
        straight.

Lie about everything, politicize it all,
Inaugural attendance, Southern border wall,

Ventilators, masks, viral tests and transmission,
Windmills, climate change, and fossil fuel emission,

Medical research, healthcare, beans, emoluments,
White supremacists, Confederate monuments,

Verbosity Constrained

The post office, voting, by mail, and in person,
And hurricane maps, presidentially worsened,

Suspiciously awarded federal contracts,
Criminal investigations, tracing contacts,

Hydroxychloroquine, social media rage,
Congressional oversight, and kids in a cage,

Journalistic murder, bibles, trips to the beach,
Inspectors General, hats, plastic straws, and bleach,

Scientific research, intelligence reports,
Nepotism, Secret Service use of resorts,

Racism, tax returns, holidays, you name it.
If you can't control it, make sure to defame it.

Outrageous behavior's excellent distractions
Might serve to conceal illegal interactions.

If that doesn't work, if some people aren't so dumb,
Keep the outrage coming, so fast their minds go
        numb.

Support sanctimonious televangelists,
Murderous dictators, armed White supremacists,

Police with rubber bullets, tear gas, swinging clubs,
Pandemic surge governors opening their pubs,

Relatives in business, Russian condo buyers,
Numerous attorneys, climate change deniers,

Blatant misogynists, sycophantic anchors,
Conspiracy theories, avaricious bankers,

Anti-vaxxers, wealthy pedophiles with boners,
Law-flouting sheriffs, and, of course, major donors.

Trash talk refuters of that Alabama "storm,"
GI's wounded, captured, killed, while in uniform,

Porn stars, playmates, fixers, former staffers who
        talk,
Gold Star families, and those with ethics who balk.

Surround yourself with Whites (their noses must be
        brown).
Pick a token Black or two. Keep the rest all down.

Make sure to pull out of the WHO,
Nuke deals, climate treaties, maybe even NATO.

Always take the credit. Don't ever take the blame.
Call all your opponents some juvenile name.

Terminate environmental regulation.
Fuck irreversible climate devastation.

Ignore every single expert: scientific,
Medical, espionage, ethics, pandemic.

Gas peaceful protesters, then pose with a bible.
Divide the country. Make everyone go tribal.

Ignore GRU bounties on US GI's,
Then suck up to Putin. Believe transparent lies.

Deny that you're a racist, but don't let them vote.
Deny you ever said it, faced with your own quote.

Commute or pardon criminal aids for silence.
Praise savage police. Relish needless violence.

It's true if you say so, and that makes it a fact.
Double down when called out. Don't ever retract.

Kidnap protesters using unmarked cops and vans.
As part of law-and-order re-election plans.

Undermine COVID mask and distance adherence.
Request and accept election interference.

Call climate change a hoax, and watch the country
      burn.
Take away a press pass. Hide every tax return.

If someone wants your ear, they'll stay at your hotel,
Tee up on your course, rent a cart, or go to hell.

They'll buy a MAGA hat, they're still in stock, ya see,
To prove that they'll support the kakistocracy.

Favors sold all require massive contribution.
Anyone objecting faces retribution.

Dictionary dot com says trumpery means trash.
And it's worse in proportion to the flow of cash.

Milk that putrescent swamp. Continue stoking fears.
Somehow con the voters to give you four more years.

July, 2020

To Make a Long Story Short

Bible, Cheap - Used only as prop.

Check all scruples at the door.

Crystal Clear

"The food, the suite, and the girls were satisfactory?"
"Even better than usual."
"To work, then. Your assignment will be to fracture their society along racial, religious, and economic lines. We will assist your infiltration into the highest levels of government. Your compensation will be enormous, via German banks. Your responsibilities are clear, Agent 45?"

International Trade

To the Editor, El Adelantado de Segovia, Segovia, Spain:

I read recently that some citizens of Segovia object to plans to install a statue of a smiling devil taking a selfie. I understand that a local legend tells about the devil building the aqueduct in exchange for the soul of a young girl, but was then tricked, and in the end did not get her soul.

I am also told that the devil manifests himself in many forms, and that he is usually the tricky one. Imagine, if you can, that he has tricked his way into the presidency of a large and powerful country, supported brutal dictators, promoted violence, did not condemn the assassination of journalists, and destabilized the entire world. I would gladly trade my devil for yours.

Thank you very much.

Un Gringo, USA

The Envelope, Please

"You're on in five minutes, sir."
"Make it ten. I haven't had time to prepare. It's been one crisis after another, without much sleep in between. I don't have any notes. I don't even have any paper."
"All I have is a used envelope, sir."
"That'll have to do... 'Four score and seven years ago...'"

Let's Not Go Through This Again, Sir

"Yes, sir, I do know who I'm talking with."

...

"As mentioned earlier, sir, we do not tolerate that type of malicious, hateful, inflammatory content."

...

"No, sir, you will not be permitted to open yet another account."

...

"We always know within the first few tweets, sir."

...

"I'm sure it's huge, sir. Will that be all, sir?"

Legal Discovery

"I heard Isaac Newton discovered the Law of Gravity while in isolation for plague in the sixteen hundreds. I wish I was accomplishing something while in isolation for this pandemic. What've you been doing?"
"Following the news. And discovering the Law of Depravity: If you think you can't possibly be more disgusted, watch tomorrow's news."

Scrape It Off Your Boots

First it wasn't what it was. That's what we were told.
Then it wasn't what it is. Somehow, we were sold.
It wasn't what it was. It isn't what it is.
Now it never even was. Logic? He's a whiz.

MULTIFACETED CHALLENGES

Choices, Bad Choices, and...

"But next weekend's the..."
"I can't go anyplace but school and piano for three weeks."
"What did she say?"
"She screamed and cried, like, forever."
"What did Dad say?"
"Sometimes it's hard to know what's right, but sometimes it's easy. And if I know I'm making bad choices, to at least make better bad choices."

Purpose

"You've got everything going for you! Everything! You're young! Healthy! Educated! And you're doing nothing!"
"You've taught me that prayer is important. And that everything in life has a purpose."
"And what's your purpose in life? What?!?!"
"Maybe my purpose in life is to make sure you don't run out of things to pray for."

Taking Control

"Why are you here?"
"I feel like an ant on a sidewalk, about to be crushed under the boots of hypocrisy. Like a jack rabbit about to be splattered by a truckload of ignorance. I'm here because I feel this is the best way to take control of my own life."
"Excellent. Welcome to kindergarten."

STRICTLY BUSINESS

Acardia

"The decedent left neither will, nor estate documents. The probate court will determine the final disposition of all the decedent's assets, which will remain frozen until such determination has been made."

"The decedent?!?! This terminology is inapplicable!"

"You will refer to the decedent as such in my court, Counselor. We have a death certificate filed by a licensed physician."

"A physician with absolutely no business…"

"To the contrary, physicians have ethical obligations in certain extreme circumstances. The certifying physician had business in the decedent's customer service department, became involved, and found no evidence of cardiac activity."

"Of course there was no evidence of cardiac activity! The decedent never had a heart! The decedent was a hundred billion dollar corporation!"

"The counselor might have kept this absence of a heart in mind during previous arguments that this corporation was a person. Next case!"

The Part Hollywood Forgot to Show You

"Drop it! An' reach for the sky!"

"Yes, ma'am… Don't shoot. There was a bounty on his head, dead or alive."

"Well, ya didn't have to shoot him in my saloon. I try to keep this place clean. You men! You ain't collectin' no bounty until you drag him outside an' mop up this mess."

Vary Charming

"You get paid to go on dates? You're... what? A male escort? A gigolo?"

"No, I usually try not to become sexually involved with the wives of my clients."

"The wives of your clients? You break up marriages professionally?"

"No. I save them."

"OK, explain."

"Suppose a guy has a wife who complains about him nonstop. Maybe he wonders if she's looking around, or worries that she might even be considering a divorce. I learn a little bit about her, just happen to run into her a few times, turn on the charm, maybe go on a couple dates. If she starts to get interested, it's easy. All I have to do is be myself. Then she'll dash for the door, and realize that maybe he's not so bad after all."

"How much do you charge? And could I tell you about my wife?"

Next Order of Business

"They're becoming dangerous!"

"They're killing each other for their gods. What'll they do to us?"

"What can they do to us? They're still using nuclear weapons."

"Their interplanetary travel is still crude."

"They're investigating wormholes!"

"It's time to intervene!"

"Most of them don't even believe we exist."

"Redirect one asteroid, done!"

"Enough! Let's vote!"

Is He Properly Qualified?

"Have you read this letter of recommendation? 'First in his MBA class'... 'charged eleven times, never convicted'... 'uses truth like a gourmet chef sprinkling spices, just enough to make things interesting'.... 'pilfered church collections and had sex with nuns as an altar boy'... 'sold his own mother'... Gentlemen, I believe we've found our next CEO!"

Sign Here

"Your independent unpublished study claims that production at our new $3 billion facility will cause 20,000 downstream cancers over the next 10 years."
"Also, thousands of strokes, heart attacks, and birth defects."
"We need a new Research Director. The 10 year package includes $2 million annually, profit sharing, and nondisclosure."
"4 million."

Trick or Treat

"I've directed 13 horror films, and last night's opening was unprecedented. 27 people across the country were taken from theaters, by ambulance, to emergency rooms, with chest pain.   Now every theater in the country is sold out for the next four weeks."
"That new marketing guy is an absolute genius! Those 27 people were actors."

Deeply Concerned, Until Monday

"Hello."
"Hi. I'm running late. I've got about a foot of wet, heavy snow to shovel before I can come in."
"Oh, no, you don't! My boys will do it. You're working this weekend, starting at noon today. The rest of us are off. If you want to have a heart attack, wait until Monday."

May Your Prayers Be Heard

"Bless me, Father, for I have sinned."
"You must pray to God for forgiveness. What have you done?"
"You know exactly what I've done, because I did it with you. Remember, I'm only twelve. You'd better pray that I don't post the videos. I'll make sure God hears your prayers for $100 a week."

Truly Valued as a Person

"You remember telling me your ex's mother paid her to divorce you, and you got nothing?"
"Sure."
"You thought my father would pay 300, maybe 400,000, if I dumped you? And you wanted half?"
"Yes!"
"He paid a million, but wanted an absolute guarantee that we're through. Your share will be one, maybe two, bullets."

In the Best Interest of All Parties

Dear Potential Plaintiff,

We were saddened to learn of your intention to hold us liable in the allegedly foreseeable death of your loved one. We know that prolonged litigation is not only costly, but also emotionally draining. For this reason, and in the best interest of all parties, except, perhaps, the decedents, we would like to assure you that all corporate assets have been moved offshore and dispersed. Our now completely worthless, anonymously and untraceably owned corporation has been dissolved. Hopefully, this will spare you the ordeal of litigation at this difficult time.

Insincerely,

Scamko

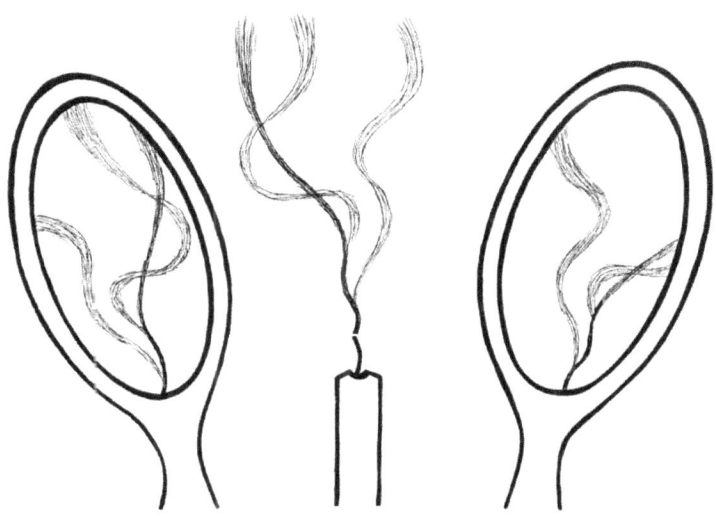

Nonstop Inspiration

"Thanks for calling Muses Unlimited. Need some inspiration?"
"I need a different muse!"
"Don't you like the inspiration you're receiving?"
"Quite the contrary! It's fantastic! My work has never been better. But it's coming 24/7! I can't sleep!"
"It sounds like you have the Economy Muse Package. Hold, please. I'll transfer you to Upgrades."

Just a Few Administrative Details

"Selling your self-published book will require state and city business licenses, with annual and quarterly filing and payments, a fire department safety inspection before licensing, quarterly filing and payment of state, county, and city sales taxes, and my quarterly accounting fees. Questions?"
"So I'll lose less money if I give copies away for free?"

I'll Help You Keep It

"You realize all members of the Order take a vow of silence."
"Yes, Abbot."
"I understand you previously broke such a vow."
"They said no one would ever know about that!"
"My brother ran that organization until you talked. Now he's on Death Row. The wine you just drank will ensure your silence this time."

**BUT WAIT!
THERE'S
MORE!**

See You Later

I never thought about reincarnation. Or hawks. Why would I? Or my wife, apparently. But she did get my attention when I walked in on her and my neighbor. A few minutes of crushing chest pain, and that was that. In retrospect, maybe things weren't so good.

My first memory in this life is of my mom feeding me pieces of squirrels and mice. Then, later, flying, and catching my own. But by the time I was about two years old, everything from my previous human life started coming back. I'd never believed in reincarnation, never took it seriously. It was just nut jobs on talk shows. You became either a more advanced or less advanced creature next time, depending on how good or bad you were. Right. So now I'm a hawk, and every year my mate and I nest pretty close to my previous human home. I think I moved up, not down, in becoming a hawk. There's no mortgage, no car payments, no committee meetings, no lies. My mate and I are very compatible.

There used to be a loud, obnoxious guy across the street, parties until 3 AM, and so on, until he wrapped his sports car around a tree. I'm pretty sure he's now that squirrel who lives in what used to be my oak tree. Same personality. Once in a while I grab him by the neck and fly him high enough for a long, steep dive.

My old neighbor still spends a lot of time with my former wife, even does chores around the house. He just now got the shorter of two extension ladders out of the garage, and leaned it against the second story part of the roof. Personally, I'd have chosen the longer ladder there. It's a little risky making the transition to and from that part of the roof when using the shorter ladder. There's a much greater risk of falling. Especially if a hawk happened to dive into him at just the right moment. This might mean I have to come back as a squirrel, or maybe even a human, next time. But it'll be worth it. Gotta go!

Undo Unto Others

"Can I help you?"
"I don't know. I hope so. I was dead, but I was retroactively baptized, then listed on your website as a Mormon in Heaven. Later, someone went to the Make a Dead Mormon Gay website and... I love your shirt, by the way. Can I go back to just being dead?"

ICE CREAM, CAKE, AND JUST DESSERTS

I Scream, You Scream

"Daddy, Jimmy's a cheater!"

"We don't call names, Honey."

"He's not being fair! Mommy said we should always be fair!"

"And we should. What happened?"

"We started a lemonade stand. We aren't both there all the time, because of soccer, and baseball, and piano, so whoever is there more gets more money."

"That sounds fair."

"He says he should get more money for every hour than I do! Even though we both do the same thing! We both squeeze lemons, and add water and sugar. And I showed him how!"

"That doesn't sound fair. Why does he say that?"

"He says he should be paid more because he's a boy. He says a lot of grownups work for you, and he says you pay the boys more than the girls. You don't do that, do you Daddy?"

"Well, I, uh, uh, uh... Who wants ice cream?"

Philosophically Incompatible with Marie Antoinette

"I appreciate your squeezing me in on such short notice. Your waiting room is packed, even at 3 o'clock on Friday afternoon."

"It's been hectic ever since I opened the practice last month. The next nearest dentist is a hundred miles away. The receptionist said you have an abscessed molar."

"It's always gotten better with antibiotics before, but I don't have any of those, and it's really bad this time. It wasn't too bad the first couple days, but it started throbbing this morning. I'd have come in sooner, but I got tied up at my bakery all day after I refused to take an order for a wedding cake. Reporters from all over the country started calling, and I spent hours giving them phone interviews. There were even a couple of film crews that showed up. But I got even. One of my buddies is a judge. I got the names of the guy and his fiancé from the order form and filed a restraining order against both of them."

"Why? Was the guy combative or something?"

"No. He was actually polite and soft spoken. But he wanted the decoration on top of the cake to be two guys in tuxedos and top hats. Two guys! Now, how about my abscess?"

"I'm afraid the situation is more complex than you realize. One option is to refer you to another dentist. Another option is for you to..."

"Wait a minute! You haven't even looked into my mouth yet, the other dentist is a hundred miles away, and it's 3 o'clock on Friday afternoon!"

"Another option is for you to get your buddy, the judge, to cancel the restraining order you filed this morning against my fiancé and me."

Appropriate Registration

"Hi! Are you registered to vote?"
"You're one of them, huh? Go back where you came from!"
"I'm from here. And I hope every citizen will vote."
"You people are trouble makers. Go register voters in Hell!"
"I'm more concerned with registrations here right now. But I'm sure you'll be able to register there someday."

This Press Conference Is Over

"Senator, that was the least responsive response that even you have ever made. I asked you about your consistent pattern of treating women as second-class citizens, allegedly for religious reasons, including your refusal to be alone with any woman other than your wife, despite your professional responsibilities. I asked about your efforts to ban abortion, to cut..."
"Our time is up. This press conference is over. Thank you all for coming."
"Senator."
"Mike! I appreciate your article yesterday. Page one! Nice work!"
"Thank you. I'm hoping you can spare a few minutes later today to review your new legislative package."
"Absolutely. My assistant can tell you where I'm booked for dinner. Perhaps you'll join us."
"Perfect, Senator! Thanks!"

Don't Answer That

"So here's the situation. Our undercover guy was watching that corner, see? Methamphetamine and prostitution. You with me?"

"Don't answer that."

"He saw you with this working woman, so to speak, on your arm. Our officer saw you punch this lady right in the face. You did that, right?"

"Don't answer that."

"She's got a broken nose. And she's got some meth, too. You know anything about where she got that?"

"Don't answer that."

"She says she got it from you, as payment for something she agreed to do for you."

"This is preposterous! My client knows absolutely nothing about any of this!"

"Then maybe you should tell him all about it after you see the film clip on the news, because that's all they've been showing for the last hour. Somebody got a video of the action from up real close. Oh, yeah, I almost forgot. There's a reporter out there who says she knows how much you like being on page one. She says you didn't have time to answer her questions this morning. She wonders if maybe..."

"Don't answer that."

They're Wrong!

"We can't afford to lose any more advertisers, so I may have to bleep some of your so-called free speech. Here's our first caller."

"I wanna warn everybody about them genetic spit tests. They say I'm 16% (bleep)! And 14% (bleep)! And... Gotta go! There's a (bleep) cross burning in my yard!"

AND APPLE PIE

Tick, Tock

"Yes, I do know that I'm not getting any younger. Yes, I do know that my biological clock is ticking. I've got to go now, Mom! Chill out, OK? Goodbye! ... I could just scream! Does your mother do that to you?"

"If all she ever did was to talk about me not getting any younger, and the ticking of my biological clock, we'd get along a lot better. Her phone messages never said 'Hi, this is Mom.' No, they said 'Tick, Tock.' So did every birthday, holiday, wedding, and anniversary card. I finally told her that if she didn't stop, I'd never speak with her again."

"And that worked?"

"That depends on whether or not you count the occasional 'Tick, Tock' billboard near my house, or the 10 second 'Tick, Tock' spots on my favorite show."

This Is Very Serious

"Social Security, Fraud Division. How can I help you?"
"I got a robocall saying that there was some kind of fraud associated with my Social Security account. It said that if I didn't call this number immediately that I might be arrested and put in jail."
"That is correct. This is very serious."
"I also heard that there's some kind of scam about Social Security fraud. This isn't one of those, is it?"
"No, ma'am. This is serious. You could be put in jail."
"For how long?"
"For 3-5 years."
''Would I have to cook or wash dishes?"
"I, uh..."
"My adult kids couldn't move in with me, could they/"
"I, uh..."
"I wouldn't have to let my husband visit me, would I?"
"I, uh..."
"Do I have to wait to be arrested, or can I just come and check in?"

Exemplification

"Doesn't that put you under a lot of pressure to behave yourself?"
"What? Being a single mom?"
"Yes. Don't you try to set a good example 100% of the time?"
"That's not realistic. I shoot for about 85%. The other 15% of the time, I show them what not to do."

It's a Relative Thing

"What are you doing?"
"I was working a crossword puzzle, until I needed a five-letter word for veracity. Now I'm online searching for the meaning of truth. Only I'm more confused than when I started."
"How so?"
"In many ways, the concept of truth is just that: a concept. Conjectures, beliefs, and emotions may come into play. It may sometimes be impossible to know what's really true, and what's not. There may be no appropriate measure or scale for some situations. Many things we can never know for certain."
"You're pondering some deep stuff."
"Deeper than an ocean basin. And I've realized that one of the only things that I absolutely know to be true is that I love you."
"Then this is a good time to tell you that Mother will be coming for the weekend."

Reader Reviews - All Purchases Verified

***** Brilliant short fiction collection! Five stars!
***** Snapshots of life in crystal clear focus!
***** Razor sharp wit!
***** So much packed into so few words!
***** Awesome dialogue!
***** I'm buying copies for all my creative writing students!
***** As concentrated as aged single malt!
***** More!
*   Do you think Mr. Author ever takes time to write to his poor mother?

A Birthday to Remember

"Are you sure this is OK?"
"My husband, kids, and grandkids are all at the lake. I had to stay behind to care for my parents. No one but you said a thing about this being my birthday. Come in."
"It's dark in here."
"Kiss me again!"
"Mmm…"
"Yeah."
"SURPRISE!!! Happy birthday to you! Happy…"

Addressing the Potential Shortfall

"Mom's become more anxious recently than usual. Even after moving to a smaller apartment, she's worried she'll outlive her savings."
"Right. She thinks there's a lot we don't tell her about our families, so she won't worry so much. She wants us to start telling her more, so she can worry herself to death sooner."

Once May Be Enough

"No fair! Hers is bigger, Mommy!"
"No! His is!"
"How can both halves be bigger? Hand them over. Hmm…. this one may be…. let me just…"
"Hey! You took a bite from mine!"
"Mmm, yummy! But now this other one's…"
"Hey! That's mine! Stop!"
"Mmm! Delicious! But now this first one's a little bigger, so…"

BANANA PEELS AND KINDERGARTEN

Banana Peel Tuesday

"Spokespersons for the White House, the Supreme Court, several senators, and numerous representatives are now reporting a total of 17 broken noses, wrists, and fingers, due to slipping and falling. The male victims were all reportedly alone with female staffers at the time of each accident. More after this message from Wonder Women Self Defense."

A Touching Story

"Welcome to kindergarten! I want to talk with you about touching. If anyone touches you where they shouldn't, tell me right away. They might say they're playing doctor."
"You mean playing movie producer?"
"Playing gymnastics coach?"
"Playing economy coach?"
"Playing priest!"
"Playing day care!"
"Playing newsroom!"
"Playing congressman!"
"Playing corner office!"
"No. Nobody's playing doctor."

RENEWABLE ENERGY IN ELKO

To Achieve Better Balance

I went out last night and heard the poets downtown,
Whose words brought a smile, a tear, a chuckle, and
      frown.
They spoke of sunrises, and of life on the range.
They spoke of things timeless, and they spoke about
      change,
Of magnificent sunsets, a sky full of stars,
Of camping in places with no lights, phones, or cars,
Of rounding up mavericks, and of cows giving birth.
Exceptional eloquence, yet still down to earth.
With a smile on my face, shortly after the show,
I felt a hand on my arm. A voice said "Don't go."
I turned, curious, to see who'd made this request,
My mind still faraway after roaming the West.
Then the next words I heard were a shock to my ear.
"You read some work of your own. Open mic, last
      year."
I've got to admit, I was totally flattered.
At last! Somebody felt that my writing mattered!
She wanted to know, had I brought anything new.
If so, was I willing to come share it with you.
I said "Everyone here has maximum talents."
She said "We need you to achieve better balance.
The rest have depth, intelligence. Some folks could
      drown.
So I'm counting on you. I know you'll dumb it down."

Feedback, Open Mic, Alternate, Friday at Noon

Peacefully sleeping, dreaming, halfway through the
      night,
When my unbidden muse said to get up and write.
I tried to resist. See, the hour was early.
My muse was insistent, then pushy and surly.
Any chances of sleeping more that night were shot.
The clock by the bed said it was three on the dot.
So I got up and scribbled. Words started to flow
About change and things timeless and life on the go.
When I read it to others, and hoped they'd say "Like!"
They all said "It's perfect to read at Open Mic!"
I went to the signup, got an alternate spot.
"Two choices: Take it or leave it. That's all we've
      got."
At check-in, the timekeeper said "Here's how it's run:
I'll signal at four minutes, five, six, then you're done."
The timekeeper, unnoticed, far off to the side,
Might have gotten more compliance if she had died.
The... moderator... pondered... over... every... word...
No hasty introduction that session was heard.
Some poets ran over, but none came even close
To the master of windbags, to Mister Verbose.
At four minutes came a subtle timekeeper hint.
The poet was barely warming up to his stint.
She signaled five minutes. He read rhyme after
      rhyme,
And appeared unaware of the passage of time.
At six minutes, she gestured "Done." He didn't look.
Was he really intending to read a whole book?
Eight minutes, it was obvious. I knew the score.
I should have taken a seat right next to the door.
He droned on six minutes, seven, eight, and then nine.
I knew there was no chance that I'd get to read mine.
He'd never heard about leaving them wanting more.
He hit ten minutes. Somebody started to snore.
His ten minute reading seemed to last for three days.
It left my mind numb and put my brain in a haze.

At session's end, the timekeeper left us no doubt.
Timid church mouse no more: "You've all got to get
       out!"
I mentioned his excess to the long droning whiz.
He was glad for my chance to hear each word of his.
A volunteer said "Those in charge want to know it,"
Said I should comment, after all, I'm a poet.
So this is my feedback, right here, in black and white.
Please don't reproduce it, as it's my copyright.
If someone's oblivious, as he seemed to be,
Shouldn't timekeepers sit where the poets could see?
And suppose one ignores each gesturing finger,
Appearing intent on indefinite linger?
When six minutes pass, before he flips the next page,
Roll a windmill on wheels right in front of the stage.

STICK TO YOUR GUNS

The Primary Objective

"Perimeter sweep completed. State your position. Over."

"Roger. Position Alpha. Awaiting orders for infiltration. Over."

"Copy. Possible hostiles at Position Delta. Repeat. Possible hostiles at Position Delta. Body armor mandatory. Do you read? Over."

"Roger. Possible hostiles at Position Delta. Body armor deployed. Awaiting orders. Over."

"Copy. Will maintain Position Beta for possible neutralization of hostiles. Over."

"Roger. You will maintain Position Beta for possible neutralization of hostiles. Awaiting orders. Over."

"Copy. Limit mission to primary objective only. Repeat. Primary objective only. No collateral objectives. Over."

"Roger. Limit mission to primary objective only. Awaiting orders."

"Copy. Proceed to Position Charlie for purchase of toothpaste and bubblegum. Over."

4th Grade Update

"Is that a real gun?"

"My dad uses the same password for everything, even his gun safe."

"Cool!"

"Mrs. Johnson won't think so. She flunked me on that spelling test yesterday. After that Jimmy tripped me on the playground. April and Tommy laughed at me. None of them will be laughing today at recess."

Those People Are Crazy

"You see this? Suicide bombing in Pakistan, 117 people killed at a wedding. Those people are crazy! And they still let 'em have dynamite! Ready for me to ring you up?"
"Yeah."
"OK... bulletproof hoodie... tactical vest... AR-15... extended magazines... Anything else?"
"No."
"Got weekend plans?"
"Something with lots of people. Maybe a big wedding."

Click

"...active shooting in progress. Live footage..."
Click.
"...death toll exceeds all previous..."
Click.
"...thoughts and prayers are with the victims and their..."
Click.
"...is not the time to politicize..."
Click.
"...RA will not issue a statement at this..."
Click.
"...Book of World Records says it will not begin tracking..."
Click.
"Babe! What's for dinner?"

IN THE BLINK OF AN EYE

Becoming One with Nature

When life overwhelms, I backpack into a remote
wilderness. Alone, there's time to ponder the infinite.
The finite. Time. Evolution. Beginnings. Endings.
Life. Death. Every creature has evolved into its
niche. Like the ram that butted me off the steep
mountainside. Like the flies that feed on my wounds.
Like the vultures that circle overhead.

Grappling with Loss

"How's your book coming?"
"It's almost done, but something completely
unforeseen and terrible has come up. Do you
remember the story I wrote a couple months ago
about a solo backpacker who falls off a mountain?
Then becomes philosophical about the situation while
waiting to die?"
"Yeah. I liked it. When you read it to me at the time,
you said you'd been inspired by having done a lot of
solo backpacking yourself, right? And you've already
included it in the manuscript, haven't you? So, what's
come up now?"
"It just hit home, hard. A friend solo backpacking
died last weekend when he fell off a mountain."
"I'm sorry."
"At least he died quickly, according to some other
hikers were nearby. Everyone will miss him, but at
least we know he didn't suffer for long."
"How are you coping with the loss?"
"Sometimes it helps for me to write about things."
"What will you write?"
"This.

NEWS WITH IMPACT

It's Not a Sign of Weakness

"I just had a weird conversation with the old guy next door."

"Like the one I had with his wife this morning?"

"What'd she say?"

"They had a lot of trouble about 40 years ago, screamed a lot, and almost got divorced. They had counseling, and they've been fine ever since. She said it's not a sign of weakness to ask for help. She said we're a wonderful young couple."

"He said pretty much the same thing. I said thanks, that I was glad they were OK, and that they're great neighbors. What else could I say?"

"Not much. I wonder why they brought that up?"

"No idea. Want a beer?"

"Sure, thanks. Want to watch the news?"

"OK."

"... fake news media is the enemy of the people!"

"YOU LYING SACK OF SHIT!"

"ASSHOLE! I HATE YOU!"

"NO! DON'T THROW THAT BOTTLE!"

"We'll return after these messages."

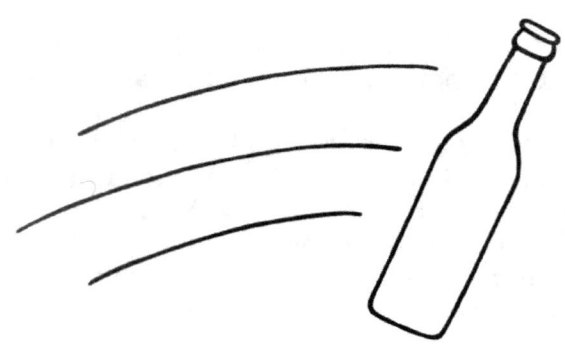

Operators Are Standing By

"If you, or someone you know, has been injured in a personal assault on a television, computer, or cellphone, while watching a presidential news clip, call the number on your screen."

"If you, or someone you know, has suffered chest pain, a heart attack, panic, anxiety, nausea, vomiting, or diarrhea, while watching a presidential news clip, call the number on your screen."

"If you, or someone you know, has destroyed or damaged a television, computer, or cellphone while watching a presidential news clip, call the number on your screen."

"You may be eligible to join the largest class action lawsuit in history. Call the number on your screen now! Operators are standing by!"

The Most Surprising Revelation

"Perhaps the most surprising revelation to come out of the long-awaited release of the presidential tax returns is the substantial investment in major electronics manufacturers."
"Electronics? Really?"
"Yes, in particular, manufacturers of televisions, small computers, and cellphones. Sales of these devices have all increased substantially since the election. Share prices of the manufacturers have reflected the increased sales."
"Any idea what's driving the uptick?"
"It was initially felt that the average household now had twice the number of these devices as before the election."
"Initially felt? But they don't?"
"No, they don't. It turns out that people are just replacing devices that they, themselves, have unintentionally destroyed in anger while watching presidential news clips."

Yet Another Approach to Testing

"Millions of Americans have gotten emails claiming that they will receive a free Coronavirus test if they send a fecal specimen in the mail. More than a million have reportedly done so. The White House has issued a statement that this is not true, and asked that people stop sending specimens to the White House."

GUY STUFF

I'll Be Right Here

"What in the hell do you want?"

"Uh, maybe I called at a bad time. I can call back later. This is…"

"I know who this is, asshole! Your name's on my phone. What?"

"You sound angry. I'm sorry if…"

"Listen to you! Mr. Effing Sensitive!"

"I know you're trying to provoke me. I'm not…"

"Right. Unless I mention…"

"Please, just stop."

"Or what? Or you're gonna come over here and punch me out? Come on! I'll be right here, asshole!"

"I'm not taking the bait. My wife let me move back in with her and the kids last month."

"So you want, what? A medal?"

"No. They're all the reward I'll ever need. I got my old job back, too. I'm controlling my anger. I couldn't have done it without you. I can't thank you enough."

"Hey, that's why I'm here. Thanks for the call."

Still Early in the Game

"It looks like you've got a new woman in your life. I've seen you with her several times now. How's that working out?"

"Really well. But there's one thing about her that I may never get used to."

"What's that"?

"She's sane."

"Don't worry too much about that. She probably still thinks you are, too."

I Sure Appreciate This

"9-1-1 Emergency Operator. Can I help you?"
"I sure hope so!"
"Sir, I hear someone screaming. Is anyone hurt?"
"No, not yet, but..."
"Is anyone in danger?"
"Not if I get out of here before your crew shows up."
"Sir, who is screaming? And why?"
"Well, my wife went out with the girls, and probably had a drink or three. And I might have forgotten to put the seat down before I went to sleep, maybe."
"Sir, is your wife stuck in the toilet?"
"See, I tried to get her out, but she might have gained just a little bit of weight these last couple of years. Not enough that any husband in his right mind would ever mention, but she woke me up with all her screaming, and maybe I said something I shouldn't have. After she threw the bathroom scale at me, I said I'd be glad to buy a new one that went up higher if that would help. That didn't seem to help. So I told her that she looked even better than before, because all that extra fat made the wrinkles harder to see. I guess maybe that wasn't the best thing to say, either. Anyhow, we're on School Street, right next to the school. I'll leave the porch light on, and the front door open. I sure appreciate this. Bye."

What More Could He Possibly Do?

"The hospital! What happened?"
"She was vacuuming. The vacuum cleaner cord got wrapped around her foot. She tripped, landed on the edge of the coffee table, and broke five ribs. Her husband really stepped up to the plate, though."
"What'd he do?"
"Before she got out of the hospital, he bought her a cordless vacuum."

Not This Time!

"If it was any other genetic condition, you'd be compassionate and empathetic. You'd be organizing support groups, raising awareness, promoting fundraisers, recruiting celebrities, lobbying legislators, writing guest editorials. Instead, you're constantly complaining about the afflicted, bashing them! I never saw this coming! You knew before we got married that I had a Y chromosome!"

Aroma Therapy

"That was an awesome backpacking trip! Six days of... Ugh! Roll down the windows! Those socks are disgusting!"
"Sorry. I forgot to pack extras. I'll toss 'em."
"No, wait! Put 'em in this plastic bag."
"Why?"
"Gordon couldn't come, but he shouldn't have to miss these. I'll slip 'em behind his filing cabinet tomorrow morning."

This May Still Be Too Subtle

"Thanks for coming! It's good to see you."
"Sure. We can't stay at my place all the time."
"Can I help carry anything in?"
"Just this."
"A present, all wrapped up... and a card... for me!"
"Open it."
"The card says 'You are such a guy!'"
"Open the package."
"It's... rags... cleanser... a toilet brush?"

Comprehensive Security System

"This place is disgusting! Dirty clothes, dishes, and garbage everywhere! I thought when you got your own place you'd finally start to clean up. You're even worse now than you were at home!"

"Mom, this is my security system. Nobody will ever break in when the place looks like this."

"You'll never get a girlfriend to come over here, either!"

"You don't know what women my age are like these days. If I invite someone over here and the house is clean, she'll start pressuring me to get married."

"That's exactly what you need! Clean this place up, find a nice girl, and invite her over for dinner."

"No way! Then she'll expect me not only to marry her, but to cook and clean, too, with absolutely no respect or appreciation, and just use me as a sex toy."

Maybe We'll Work on Those Things

"You've recently learned that you have an adult daughter and she's coming to visit. You're puzzled by my indifference. Look, you've never helped her with things like walking. She's never even thrown up on you."

"I didn't realize how important those things are. Before she gets here, I'll buy enough tequila that both could happen."

MEMORY LANE

His Name Is Charlie

"Nine One One Emergency Operator. Can I help you?"

"There's a man in my house!"

"Are you in any immediate danger?"

"I don't think so. Not right now."

"Is he armed?"

"Not that I can see."

"Can you get away?"

"Why should I have to leave? It's my house!"

"What's he doing?"

"He's in a chair in the living room. He's snoring."

"What's your address?"

"Umm..."

"What's your name?"

"Umm..."

"Is this Ellie?"

"I believe so, yes."

"Is the man wearing a blue flannel shirt?"

"Yes! He is!"

"His name is Charlie. He's your husband."

Memory Enhancement

"No! Please! I have a wife! Kids!"

"I know."

"I've told you everything!"

"I don't think so. But I know how to, let's say, improve your memory a little bit, keep the conversation flowing."

"No! OK! Maybe I remember a couple more things. What do you want to know?"

"Let's start with the itemized deductions."

DON'T TRY THIS AT HOME!

Remember Who the Boss Is

"Bob asked me to come over here, pick you up, and take you back to town. In the twelve years I've worked for him, I've never seen him so mad. What happened?"

"He made a little mistake."

"He's not this mad over just a little mistake. Something else happened. What?"

"Working with him isn't like working with you or the other guys. You know how it is on these farm surveys. Just two guys, driving out to the job and back to town together, working together all day, even having lunch together in some small-town diner."

"Sure. That's how it is."

"So, it's normal to talk once in awhile, right? But mostly if he's talking he just tells little stories, and every single one of them is about the same thing. It's important to remember who the boss is. Anything else he might have to say usually implies that I'm the dumbest person who's ever been born. Everything always has to be perfect, which I totally understand, and it always has to be faster, faster, faster."

"Well, he is the boss."

"And it's important to remember who the boss is. He's been very clear on that, all day, every day, every time I've had to work with him."

"So, what happened?"

"You know how, when I'm working with you, and we're having lunch in some diner, sitting across the table from each other, you review the plans for the afternoon, do calculations, and jot down tables of numbers while you're eating?"

"Yeah, sure, then it's already done when we get back to work."

"And I glance at what you're doing, upside down,

76

from across the table, and occasionally suggest that you recheck one of the numbers?"

"Yeah. I don't know how you do that. You're not even a surveyor, and you've only been on the job for a few months. But it's helpful. Thanks."

"You're welcome. I'm glad to help. I do that when I work with the other guys, too, and they they're appreciative, too. Except Bob, who frequently implies that I'm stupid. I quit doing that for him."

"So, what happened?"

"Today we were doing a survey for a new subdivision, marking street center lines, property corners, easements, the usual. This has been one of the hottest, most humid days all summer. The soil was hard, dry clay. We did a lot of measurements, and I marked the points with nails and bright plastic ribbon, like usual. Then I had to go back, drive an oak stake at each point, and tie a ribbon onto each stake, like usual."

"So, what happened?"

"I got a quick peek at the plans during lunch. Bob made a little mistake with the calculations for one of the first points we had to set, and everything that followed was wrong. Everything. Due to the complexity of the layout, every point was off by a different amount. Driving each stake into the dry hardpan clay with a sledgehammer took so long that I had time to calculate, in my head, exactly how far off each point was from where it was supposed to be. It was hot, sweaty, miserable work, but I did it with a smile, hoping I'd get a chance to enjoy discussing the situation with Bob later."

"And you did."

"Three hours into it, he finally told me to stop driving stakes. He said he thought there might be something wrong, and that he had to recheck everything. That's when I told him exactly how far off that particular point was from where it was supposed to be. And that I remembered exactly who the boss was."

Enjoy It While It Lasts

"Hello."
"Hi. The plumbing is all done. You can use the bathrooms, the kitchen, the laundry, everything."
"That's great! Thanks!"
"I'll come by in the morning to pick up a check."
"This gives me a very warm, peaceful feeling."
"Having plumbing that works?"
"No. The fact that someone will actually care if I die tonight."

Naughty or Nice?

"Look in the bag. It's all there: your fishing rod, Janet's earrings, Tommy's video games, Mary's skates."
"You've lost weight. Since when does Santa weigh 160 pounds?"
"Since my gastric bypass. You remember that shotgun I brought you last year? You'll be on the Naughty List if you don't point it someplace else real soon."

How Many?

"Would you please repeat back to me what I've told you?"
"You've already told me several times."
"True. And you've told me several times that you understand. But, despite my asking, you have not repeated it back to me, even once."
"Sir, I speak six languages."
"Impressive! In how many of them do you listen?"

Consider All the Angles

The Kevlar shirt, pants, and jacket looked just like regular clothes, but could stop anything they might be carrying today. Take no chances, not anymore. He felt the metal barrel in his pocket. He was ready. Turning to face them, he pulled the chalk holder from his pocket. "Today we'll discuss the geometry of triangles."

Relevant Experience

"I need you to write something else for our newest project."
"I turned in the revised specs yesterday."
"This'll be different. An entertaining short story related to the project will stir up even more team spirit."
"I'm a technical writer. I don't write creative fiction."
"Really? Go back and reread your own annual self evaluations."

It's a Matter of Degree

"No kidding? You're a PhD, too?"
"Philosophy, Harvard, 1979. And you?"
"English Lit, Princeton, 1984. Would you like some more of this wine, Doctor? A bit immature, perhaps, but impressive plasticity."
"Splendid, thanks. Any thoughts of retirement?"
"No, I'd miss it. I'll be back on my off ramp with my sign tomorrow."
"Yeah, me, too."

Halfway There

Truly impressive negligence,
Paired with complete incompetence.
Why spend the time to do it right?
When they find out, you're out of sight.
Major details? You just skip 'em.
Middle fingers? Sure, just flip 'em.
Criticize? You just ignore it.
Reputation? Can't restore it.
Working hard? Just pick a topic.
Greatest efforts? Microscopic.
Conscientious? There's not a trace.
I don't know how you show your face.
Any complaints? You go stone deaf.
Then we all say "Dubya T F?"
You always pick the half-assed way.
The rest of us around you pay.
You've redefined bare minimum.
I'm working 'til it leaves me numb.
Your work ethic has up and quit.
It's clear that you don't give a shit.
Your goal's to work fast. You don't care
That you just end up halfway there.
You're skeptical? Pass this around.
Then put your ear down to the ground.
Without you life will be deluxe,
Cuz working with you really sucks.
More work with you? Just can't buy it.
Starting on a shit-free diet.

 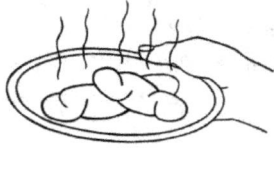

Details, Details...

"Have you killed anyone before?"
"No, but I can handle this."
"Are you going to write about it afterwards? It'll be a real life-changing experience."
"You think I should?"
"Are you kidding? Rejected author murders editor, then writes the story!"
"Will you help me?"
"Remember, I won't be here after you pull that trigger."

Go for It!

"Retiring? You can't retire! You're a legend around here!"
"How many more years of abuse and overwork am I supposed to take?"
"You're not old enough to retire."
"I'm old enough to die, any time. You'd better hope that I don't just drop dead right here, right now."
"Dude! That would be, like, totally cool!"

If You Put It That Way...

"This party is jam packed. I thought you said only three people were coming."
"The first invitations I sent just said this would be your retirement party. After I reworded the invitations, everybody wanted to come."
"What did you say?"
"That this was our chance to celebrate never, ever having to work with you again."

TAKE YOUR DAUGHTER TO WORK DAY

Earlier That Day

"After I vacuumed her room, I changed the sheets on the bed. I found this book right here under the mattress. I thought you might want to discuss this with her."

"Let me see... Oh, no! By page 12 there are four naked people in a hot tub! The men are fondling the women, the women are fondling each other, and my daughter's only 13! No!"

"You're crying."

"I'm getting a headache."

"Let me massage your neck... You're so tense."

"Oh, that feels good."

"Your back is also very tight Let's get your shirt and shoes off. Lie down, and I'll rub your back, too."

"Thanks. Mmm... Ooh... Aah..."

"I'm going to pause for a moment to remove a couple things myself. I'm getting warm."

"Just hold me... Yes... Yes..."

"My husband will be picking me up in twenty minutes. Would you like him to join us?"

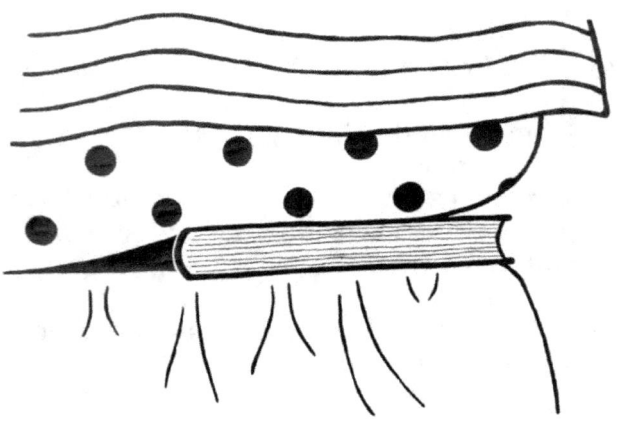

Later That Same Day

"The maid found this disgusting filth under your mattress. This is hardcore pornography! There are groups of people doing all sorts of unspeakable..."
"Come out of your shell, Mom! This isn't porno, it's erotica."
"Oh, it's erotica, is it? Well, then, classy hardcore pornography!"
"The writing is amazing. The reviewers all comment on its psychological depth and complexity."
"This is not appropriate for a young woman of 13! A feminist political canvasser and a delivery man coincidentally arrive at the Johnson residence at the same time, and, call it what you will, by page 12, they, and the Johnsons, are all naked in the hot tub. And that's just the part before the neighbors, the book club, the personal trainer, the masseuse, and all the rest of them show up!"
"You seem to know an awful lot about this book, Mom."
"There, uh, uh, was a review on the radio."

Weekly Literary Update

"This program is made possible by the generosity of our listeners. We now return to Weekly Literary Update. Professor."

"Thank you. This segment will address *And How Do You Feel About That?* by Stefan Upp, which certainly caught me off guard."

"How so?"

"I was only peripherally aware of his previous work due to its blatantly pornographic nature."

"You mean the anatomically impressive delivery man and the lonely housewife? That sort of thing?"

"Exactly. And, frankly, this story is packed with an abundance of, shall we say, adventurous group activity, but that's not what makes it so insistently compelling."

"Do tell."

"The unexpected warmth, depth, and charm of the characters, their surprising, but quite plausible virtues and flaws, the intelligence, wit, and irony of their conversations, and the all too realistic complexity of their interactions, make this far more than a masterpiece of literary erotica. Don't miss it!"

The Interview After the Sermon

"Thank you for joining us today, Reverend."

"My pleasure."

"A lot of interest has been aroused, so to speak, since your nationally televised sermon on pornography."

"That was a response to a pornographic novel topping the bestseller list."

"The critics are saying that the nonsexual content of the book is what actually makes it so compelling. The characters include a Buddhist clinical psychologist, his bipolar neurosurgeon wife, a feminist combat veteran pacifist, a poetry writing delivery man, a blind sculptor, an atheist retired astronaut, a yoga instructor CEO..."

"I'm sure the conversations at our Bible study group are every bit as stimulating."

"Have you actually read the book?"

"Quite a few copies were donated anonymously after my sermon. I found it rather difficult to read."

"Due to its disturbing content?"

"The production quality must have been rather poor. Many of the pages were stuck together."

✳✳✳✳✳✳✳✳✳✳✳✳✳✳✳✳✳✳✳✳✳✳✳✳

IMAGE DELETED
in a transient
attempt at
good taste

✳✳✳✳✳✳✳✳✳✳✳✳✳✳✳✳✳✳✳✳✳✳✳✳

And How Do You Feel About That?

"The maid found some hardcore pornography under my daughter's mattress, Doctor, and..."
"Pornography? What? Photos? Magazines?"
"A book, actually, called *And How Do You Feel About That?* It's disgusting! It's full of so much... such... it's..."
"You're obviously upset. Perhaps you'll find some consolation in that the reviewers are calling it literary erotica, rather than pornography, and that it's topping the bestseller list."
"It's filled with kinky group sex that the reader is expected to casually accept as part of an even more twisted set of complex interpersonal relationships. It's not appropriate for a young woman of 13!"
"It sounds as if you've read it yourself."
"I wrote it!"
"Our time is up, but you're my last patient of the day. If you have time, I'd enjoy discussing this with you personally, rather than professionally, right now."
"Why, yes, I..."
"Would you care for some wine?"

Speaking Personally

"So you wrote *And How Do You Feel About That?* The literary erotica that's topping the bestseller list? Really? Using a pseudonym?"
"Yes, Doctor. But I'm disgusted. My 13 year-old daughter had a copy under her mattress! I'm done! My writing career is over!"
"Please reconsider. You're an incredible writer!"
"I'm also a mother! And a televangelist with the largest congregation in the country."
"The characters and their interactions are superb! They're what really make the story. Although the variety of the explicit sexual interactions was, well... and the implicit sexual interactions! That scene with the blind sculptor who kept her long white satin gloves on the whole time, despite everything else that was happening! Genius! I had no idea you were so... adventurous!"
"I really don't know much about sex. I did most of my research online."
"I'd be willing to help you with a little research, Reverend."

Are You Awake?

"Are you awake?"
"Ugh."
"Are you awake?"
"Umm... What? It's 3 AM."
"I'm sorry. I'm worried about that presentation at work. It's ready, but I can't sleep. Hearing about the stories you're writing always helps me go back to sleep."
"Yeah, OK. Hmm... This woman's maid... tells her about finding porno under the woman's daughter's mattress. She's 13..."
"Good."
"Next thing, the woman and the maid are in the daughter's bed... maybe the maid's husband, too. Later that day, she confronts her daughter, who points out that the woman knows an awful lot about this book."
"I like it."
"And then... a rave review of the book on a talk show... Are you awake?"
"Umm."
"Maybe a televangelist giving a sermon about the evils of pornography... Oh, yeah! The woman visits her shrink, and... I love this! Are you awake? No? I've got to get up and write this down."

What're You Working On?

"That's the fourth time you've put the light on in the last hour. Another story?"
"Sorry. If I don't write some notes, I'll lose it."
"That's OK. What now?"
"You remember the other night I told you about the woman's daughter with the porno under her mattress, and the maid finds it?"
"Sure. And then the mom and the maid…"
"Yeah. It turns out the critics love the book, say it's erotica, not pornography, and it becomes a bestseller. There's a televangelist who gives a sermon condemning pornography. Then the mom sees her psychotherapist, and it turns out that the mom is not only the televangelist who gave the sermon, but, also, using a pseudonym, the author of the book. After she and the shrink get it on…"
"I love it! No wonder you can't sleep."
"But I need some sleep. Maybe if you tell me what you're doing at work…"

The Next Week

"But your writing…"

"Let me tell you about my late husband before turning to that, Doctor. He was a very spiritual man, but sometimes misunderstood. He connected with others so deeply, and so sincerely, then matched them with the absolutely perfect pre-owned vehicle. After his release from prison, he was called to the ministry. The nausea from my pregnancy kept me from working. I started writing, but couldn't get published until I stooped to writing pornography."

"So that's how…"

"Tragically, the severely troubled husband of a congregant misunderstood his wife's all-night prayer session with my husband and me. After the funeral, I was called to lead the growing congregation. As a single mother, I still needed the income from writing."

"And now you're leading the country's largest congregation. Our session time is up, but if you'd like to visit personally…"

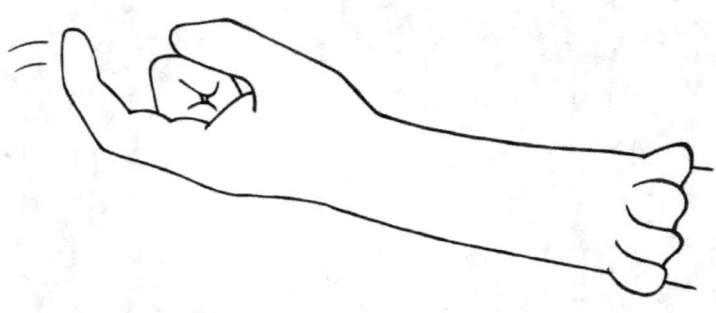

It Was to Die For

"Here, have some wine, Doctor."
"Thank you, Reverend. Those long white satin gloves you're wearing today are all I can think about! Is your wine OK? Mine tastes…"
"Mine's fine. Try some more. Oh, I got your note, saying 'I'm so sorry.' Nonsense! You were heavenly!"
"I'm sorry if I was inappropriate."
"You were very appropriate, rejoicing in the Spirit! You even yelled 'Oh, God! Oh, God!'"
"It was to die for!"
"It certainly was."
"I'm… getting… sleepy."
"Drink up! That's it! By the way, I got a blackmail note. It said if I quit writing pornography that my congregation would be informed. Now that was to die for! Say, did I mention that no one but you knew about my writing? I'll just leave this note saying how sorry you are right here, so they'll find it when they find you."

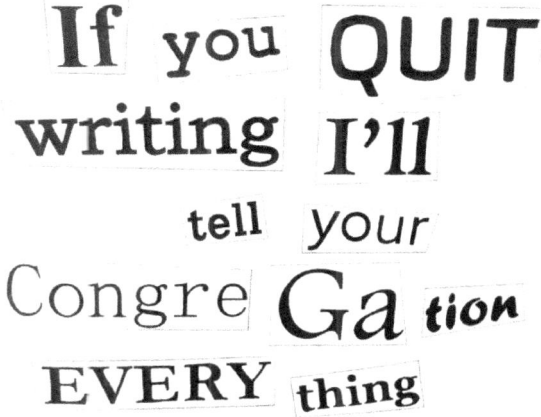

Prepping for Career Week

"Investigators have determined that the death was an intentional overdose. A note was found at the scene. In other news…"

"Honey, I'm home!"

"Hi, Mom. I'm in here."

"How was school?"

"OK. All my homework is done. Next week is Career Week."

"You're only 13, so you've still got lots of time. Do you still want to be an astrobiologist?"

"I'm thinking seriously about following in your footsteps."

"Really? Your father and I were both called to the ministry at about 30. I'll help you look into divinity schools."

"That's not what I meant, but, OK, that would be a good enough day job until my real career takes off."

"What real career?"

"Let's make a deal, Mom. I'll forget a whole bunch of things I'm not supposed to know about, and show you how to make better passwords, if you show me how to write like you do."

OLD PASSWORD   Letmein1

NEW PASSWORD   Pr3y0n5alv8t10n

RE-ENTER NEW   Pr3y0n5alv8t10n

Passing the Twisted Torch

"Honey, I've gone way beyond everything we agreed on… writing several more bestsellers, mentoring your writing, and continuing to lead the congregation. You've been out of divinity school three years. It's time for you to get your call."
"OK, OK, Mom. He's reviewing my book now. Please, let's listen."
"Her naughty protagonist peered deeply into warped nooks and crannies of my own soul that I never even knew existed. Disappointed fans of the mysterious, and even more mysteriously departed, master of literary erotica, Stefan Upp, can rejoice. The twisted torch and the kinky keyboard have now been passed to his heir apparent, Lyktu Moysen."
"Thank you, Professor. We'll return to Weekly Literary Update after these public service announcements."
"That's a wonderful review, Sweetie! Now, it's time for me to retire, and for your call to lead the congregation."

Questioning Faith

"You've been retired for a couple years now,
Mom. You seem to like it!"
"I love it! I'd have done it sooner if you hadn't…"
"I'm sorry about the blackmail. And your therapist."
"He wasn't really important. And after a few back-to-back all-night, one-on-one prayer sessions with me, the investigator was too tired to do much of an investigation. He took a quick look at the note that was left at the scene, and that was that. Writing the intellectual porno, excuse me, erotica, was fun, especially the research. As was mentoring your writing career, which seems to be going very well. But I'd had enough, and was certainly glad to hand the congregation over to you, no matter how lucrative it was. By now, I'm sure you've led thousands to eternal salvation. And banked millions offshore."
"Yes, I have, on both counts. But one thing is starting to bother me. What if there really is a god?"

A DEVASTATING PATHOGEN

Incompetence Gone Viral

These words, written early April, Twenty Twenty,
Arrive, surrounded, insanity aplenty.

Contagious COVID-19 brought us widespread death.
Stay far away. Be careful with each touch and breath.

Practice social distancing. Sew yourself a mask.
No one plans on coming in. They won't even ask.

Stay home. Isolate. They call it shelter in place.
Wash your hands obsessively, and don't touch your
         face.

How could this have happened? What say those in
         the know?
Who'll have the next body tag hanging on their toe?

Look back. Review a little bit of history.
The facts just might illuminate this mystery.

Twenty Fourteen, Ebola found us unprepared.
That time we got lucky. Yeah, that time we were
         spared.

Twenty Sixteen, scientists came up with a way
To be ready next time, limit death, save the day.

They wrote pandemic guidelines. We'd have a
         head start
Based on science and experience, every part.

Have an expert on pandemic, mass infection,
Guide the NSC, coordinate direction.

Start a global program, track new pandemic bugs,
Buy us time, manufacture new vaccines and drugs.

We'd stockpile equipment, all ready, set to go.
Vigilant and well-equipped, we'd be safe, you know?

Late in Twenty Sixteen, we saw a change in course.
Presidential tweets said the cart's before the horse.

The new guy said the last one had it all so wrong.
He'd undo it all, and it wouldn't take him long.

The pandemic expert was kicked off NSC.
Dropped the global program. Leave everything to me.

Believe me! I'm a genius! I know what to do.
I'm doing a great job. A Nobel? Maybe two.

Pandemic plans were not maintained, just retired.
Stockpiled equipment, insufficient, expired.

December Twenty Nineteen, Wuhan viral news,
Ignored and denied, despite informed expert views.

New year, Twenty Twenty, the virus hit our shore.
Epidemiologists told us what's in store.

Top White House advisors said surely this will spread.
We may see as many as half a million dead.

First, he just ignored it, then said "We're in control."
Johns Hopkins kept the count of each day's deathly
        toll.

They were low, underestimating those who die,
Missing those not tested by kits in short supply.

Testing? Why bother? This will all just go away.
Like a miracle! Who cares what those experts say?

He still played lots of golf, never missed a rally,
Minimized it all, including body tally.

Asymptomatic transmission? Huh? What's that
    mean?
Never mind, cuz it's like the flu that we've all seen.

His "Democratic hoax," spewed as his lies increased,
Won't work on certificates filed for the deceased.

Shortages of ventilators, masks, gloves, and gowns,
Cause funerary backlogs as the system drowns.

Death, exceeded only by his mendacity,
Fills morgues beyond their overflow capacity.

Bodies, filling cooler trucks, loaded to the max,
Aren't his fault. The governors are stupid. They're
    lax.

He's not responsible, only points his finger.
It's always someone else. Few staff members linger.

Now he's pushing chloroquine. Cardiac arrest?
Don't worry. Remember, his ratings are the best.

We've all heard it said, learn from the past, or repeat.
Will we now be undone by ignorant conceit?

If you've lost some loved ones, many share your
    sorrow.
He can't. Today. Or yesterday. Or tomorrow.

So we cross fingers, watching counts climb to the sky
And wonder, how many more will succumb? Will die?

One or two hundred thousand, somewhere in that
    range?
Small potatoes. Watch what he does with climate
    change.

Thus far there's been no mention of dollars or God.
Though he claims wealth, gave two Corinthians a nod.

Right from the start, he pinched pennies to save
    millions.
But inept, delayed response cost extra trillions.

Quick! Second Corinthians! Now! On the double!
Chapter One…. Oops!   Be aware of Asian trouble.

With all that's gone on, be sure that we'll remember,
He's up for re-election, this year, November.

April, 2020

Legalize Sanity

In August, Twenty Twenty, chaos runs berserk.
Raging pandemic, thirty million out of work.

With evictions, foreclosures, overdrawn accounts,
Delinquencies, bankruptcies, major havoc mounts.

Widespread reproach of harsh police brutality
Too often exposes vicious reality.

Protesters tear gassed, clubbed, abducted, arrested.
The US Bill of Rights uniquely molested.

Unbridled corruption, perpetrators set free.
Other countries watch, wondering how can this be?

The police murder Blacks, any and everywhere,
While the Whiner-in-Chief tweets his treatment's
          unfair.

Desperation, homelessness, begging in the streets,
Poverty and hunger, never found in his tweets.

In Twenty Sixteen, we all hoped for a leader.
Instead, what we got was an out-and-out cheater.

Elections, SAT scores, business, golf, the draft,
Marriage, charity, taxes, ubiquitous graft.

What's he been doing to make our crises better?
Threw the Ricans paper towels when they got wetter.

That's what they got after Hurricane Maria.
For crises since then he's dispensed logorrhea.

In the event of an historic pandemic
Infectious guidance ought not be thought polemic,

But, rather, sought, elucidated, and heeded,
Instead of backstabbed every time that he tweeted.

Follow simple guidelines. Stay apart. Wear a mask.
Wash your hands. Test and trace. Could he? Don't
        even ask.

He called it a hoax, said it would all go away.
Now a thousand more die every single sad day.

Asked why, with COVID testing, did he drop the ball?
Quote: "I don't take responsibility at all."

Many governors shut down, to keep people safe.
For their efforts received the incompetent's strafe.

Chicago economists advised they stay closed.
If you open too soon, the economy's hosed.

Five thousand COVID deaths, early April, now quaint.
The Denier-In-Chief said we can't have restraint.

Meanwhile, he claimed, the WHO blew it.
Not one more dollar, there's no way he'll renew it.

Continue COVID restrictions, said the MD's,
But the Genius-in-Chief had militants to please.

More tweets. Liberate Michigan, Minnesota,
Virginia. Intelligence? Not one iota.

As financial deficits began to balloon,
He pushed governors to reopen too soon.

No surprise, COVID deaths went up like a rocket.
Of some, all that's left is a face in a locket.

While Congress negotiated stimulus plans,
The Grifter-in-Chief promoted oversight bans.

He pushed for significant corporate bailout,
And tried to prohibit blue state ballot mail out.

Hamstrung the post office before the election
So it's harder to vote a change in direction.

Eliminate pickup boxes, sorting machines,
To slow down the mail by any possible means.

Deliberate delay of checks, medication,
Not the worst, by far, from this administration.

Spend whatever it takes on voter suppression.
No problem, despite economic recession.

To claim he's managed COVID would be quite a reach
Unless we count his push for ingestion of bleach,

And hydroxychloroquine, despite the data.
Some took it. Mortality increased pro rata.

Sixty-five thousand COVID deaths by early May
Made Columbia researchers speak up and say

There'd be much less death if we'd followed the
       science.
The Braggart-in-Chief still continued defiance.

Exit George Floyd, neck under an officer's knee,
Eight minutes, forty-six seconds, for all to see.

Minneapolis cops, murderers, all four charged,
Sparked protests, local, then global, viral, enlarged.

Oh, viral, yeah... one hundred thousand dead, late
       May,
Conspiracy theorists deny them away.

Enter the Bungler-in-Chief, needing distraction,
And determined to take executive action.

Forget viral deaths. Ignore economic woes.
Focus all attention on ever lower blows.

Brutal racist cops? No way! Don't ever buy it.
Send in the troops. Escalate. Provoke a riot.

The clubbing of looters, just as much as you please,
While it may treat some symptoms, ignores the
        disease.

To pretend looting's the biggest problem we face
Isn't just ignorance. No, it's also disgrace.

When it's inconvenient, the First Amendment's moot.
Clear Lafayette Square for a Bible photo shoot.

Nothing shouts "Praise Jesus!" like tear gas and a
        club.
He'll never understand the Nobel Peace Prize snub.

Four months with no rally, and itching for a stage,
Time to lie in Tulsa, fan flames of hate and rage.

No! Wait! It'll be a superspreader event!
His supporters and he are totally hell bent.

He brags: A million can't wait! Just six thousand
        show
After signing waivers, to agree that they know

Their hero's never at fault, he's a busy guy,
And they won't annoy him if they get sick or die.

Unmasked, packed in close, CDC guidelines in vain,
Then a month on a vent, and death for Herman Cain.

One of many Tulsa lies: COVID testing's jive.
By late June the death toll surpassed one twenty-five.

Meanwhile, in New Zealand, no cases for three
     weeks.
They listened to experts, not anti-science freaks.

The Tweeter-in-Chief's posts, blocked in violation
Of the anti-hate rules, and misinformation.

Headline in July: Russian bounties on GI's.
He ignored the briefings, took questions, spewed his
     lies.

Several new books, chock-full of juicy disclosure,
Are hitting the shelves at a time when he's so sure

He's the one, chosen by God, to confabulate
That he, only he, can make America great.

The books are by his niece, an advisor or two,
A former attorney. He says none of it's true.

There are negative ads, made by conservatives,
Jam-packed with pejorative reverberatives.

Fresh adverse rulings affect hidden tax returns
And women assaulted, who say: Time that he learns.

Volatile behaviors, growing still more poutful,
November re-election ever more doubtful.

His incompetence, subject now of scrutiny,
Craves deflection, to lessen risk of mutiny.

Roll back existing fair housing regulation,
And kneecap environmental legislation.

Fire inspectors investigating corruption,
Public service careers cut short by abruption.

Put hydroxychloroquine back on his playlist,
Now pushed by an expert on his transient A list.

An expert? You think he cares what they've got to
          say?
Sure, if they're experts on alien DNA,

Or oleandrin, for use in medication,
And nocturnal incubus insemination.

Millions uninsured, so cut options even more.
Sure, they want healthcare, but, too bad, because
          they're poor.

Confederate statues and canned beans are nifty.
As far as COVID deaths, they just hit one fifty.

With New Zealand COVID-free for one hundred days,
No fiddle, unlike Nero, golf's what this guy plays.

Marie Antoinette, unconcerned to this degree
Lost a bit of weight. Where's his driver? Where's his
          tee?

Failing payment, some face water disconnection.
He talks of showerheads, and his hair's perfection.

He brags about passing a dementia screening,
Which may be his peak intellectual leaning.

Bogus dysfunctional Executive Orders,
Other countries don't want us crossing their borders,

Alienation of traditional allies,
Gassing the Wall of Moms, and twenty thousand lies,

Threatening November election postponement,
Nocuous demeanor, but never atonement.

He's the victim of lies, abuse, personal loss,
Persecuted more than What's-His-Name on the cross.

Mid-August death toll, one seventy, not his biz.
The Dodger-in-Chief explains "It is what it is."

That's one hundred seventy thousand dead, so far.
Despite his ineptitude, he brags he's a star.

Should his next self-named tower be piles of the
      dead?
From COVID, guns, police, uninsured, underfed?

True, some may have claimed that he's not
      presidential,
But take a good look at his every credential.

He's got Herbert Hoover's fiscal ability,
Much more than Richard Nixon's culpability,

Totally on board with Andrew Jackson on race.
Bill Clinton's infidelity? Now second place.

One more former presidential comparison,
Some wish he'd copied William Henry Harrison.

Remember, he said he'd put America first.
Doubters said he wouldn't, but their bubbles have
      burst.

We're first in COVID deaths, and we're first in cases,
Far ahead of all other countries and places.

First in school shootings, yet the NRA lingers.
First in "thoughts and prayers" inspired by trigger
      fingers.

First in Black incarceration, without release,
And in murder of Blacks by on duty police.

First in contempt towards advanced education,
And leaders' scientific repudiation.

He said we'd all get sick of it, winning so much.
He nailed the sick part, plus bonus dying and such.

Hatred, greed, intolerance, all became hardwired.
Logic's out the window. Insanity's required.

For instance, consider the Psychopath-in-Chief,
Elevated far above ordinary thief.

Invariably self-congratulatory,
Followed by those sufficiently laudatory.

Forget about thought. It's all about devotion,
Adulation, or you've got the wrong emotion.

Narcissistic Personality Disorder,
Ass-kissed by every sycophantic supporter.

You want to know more? Help democracy survive?
The best insight on him's in the DSM Five,

Diagnostic and Statistical Manual
Of Mental Disorders. Take a peek, if you will,

Fifth edition, Twenty Thirteen. Diagnostic
Descriptions of him are frightfully prognostic.

If you're reluctant to crack the DSM Five,
Averse to submerge in that psychiatric dive,

Then browse Wikipedia, look up NPD,
And while you're at it, check out sociopathy.

Those who learn of this retrospectively, someday,
May wonder, was it this crazy day after day,

Into month after month, and then year after year,
A demagogue stoking hatred, anger, and fear,

Driven by ego, mental illness, vanity.
If so, why didn't we legalize sanity?

August, 2020

BUT WHO? AND WHY?

The Real Issues

I don't care what you say. I've heard it all before.
All your research and facts are no more than a bore.

You think you've spelled it all out, events and details,
But never one word about Hillary's emails,

Vaccines, autism, Q, 5G, or dogs who vote,
Birth certificates, and don't try to sugar coat

A virus that doesn't really even exist,
Though it was man-made by a deep state terrorist.

You won't change my beliefs with logic or zingers.
Try to pry them from my cold, dead, middle fingers.

I Resent the Implication!

Climate change, corruption, yada, yada, yada.
Live someplace else if your kids hit a piñata.

It's not my fault they're different, black or brown or
        poor,
But I don't want those people living right next door.

I'm no racist. I resent the implication!
If I want to see them, I'll go on vacation.

You think that I'll forget, that I won't remember,
Who'll keep them far away from me after this
        November?

Doing The Lord's Work

King David watched Bathsheba bathe. Wow! She
      was hot!
First, he had his way with her, then cooked up a plot.

She was Uriah's wife. There's no doubt David knew.
So, David had him murdered. What else could he do?

David was a sinner, but he's the one God chose.
Our president's not perfect. God already knows.

The president is always working for The Lord.
And so, The Lord provides him White House room and
      board.

When a woman's pregnant, and visits her MD,
They shouldn't have a choice. It's up to God, and me.

As far as LGBTQ, I never judge.
But God will send them straight to hell. He'll never
      budge.

This pandemic's due to their sick, perverted path,
Now all of mankind feels the pain of The Lord's wrath.

The Lord works in strange ways. Forget about your
      fears.
He wants the Sinner-in-Chief around four more years.

Help re-elect him with your generosity.
By the way, don't forget my 501(c)(3).

Simple

All those big fancy words used by that other guy
Can't change the fact that every single one's a lie.

If you wonder why I'm sure, this is how I know,
The president, on TV, said that it was so.

I get every word he says, never have a doubt.
I never have to question what it's all about.

He keeps it simple, won't waste time on facts and
        stuff,
Just gets into right and wrong. Who needs all the
        fluff?

I know that he's a genius, doing a great job,
But you'd never hear it from all the fake news mob.

It's fun when he's onstage, the energy and cheers.
It's really sad to think he'll get just four more years.

Peaceful Protest Essentials

Giant tires, lifted pickups, flapping flags fly high.
Try to stop the caravan, someone may just die.

Hawaiian shirts or camos, extra magazines,
And, most importantly, enough AR-15's.

Leave Me Out of This

I saw it on the news. It looked pretty awful.
Just lock them up if their actions are unlawful.

I don't want to get involved, don't have much to say.
Just leave me alone. Me and my 401k.

Not Gonna Happen

You try to tell me what I can and cannot do.
You think I'm gonna listen? I've got news for you.

You say I'll trash the world's future, lay it all to waste,
Claiming everything you say is all science-based.

I've worked hard all my life, and learned that
        nothing's free.
Name one thing great great grandkids ever did for
        me.

Nothing needs to change. Things are fine the way
        they are,
Except I want a new jet and a faster car.

I'm fracking for oil, so you stay out of my way.
I bought some politicians. It's called pay for play.

There's more I could tell you, but you don't want to
        hear.
There's no way in hell I'm changing my vote this year.

GRACEFULLY

90 Is the New 60

"Hello, Jimmy? It's Great Grandpa."
...
"That's good. Listen, I only get one phone call. I need a favor. There's some money under the mattress."
...
"Well, your great grandma and I went to the lake for a picnic. It was hot, and after a skinny dip, she got a little frisky. Then the ranger showed up."

The Important Stuff

"Mommy, Great Grandma Berta just told me she's really Great Grandpa Bert. And she's not a girl, she's really a boy!"
"I know, honey. If it's hard for you, it's even harder for her. I mean him. But she still loves you. I mean he."
"Will she still bake me cookies?"
"Let's ask him."

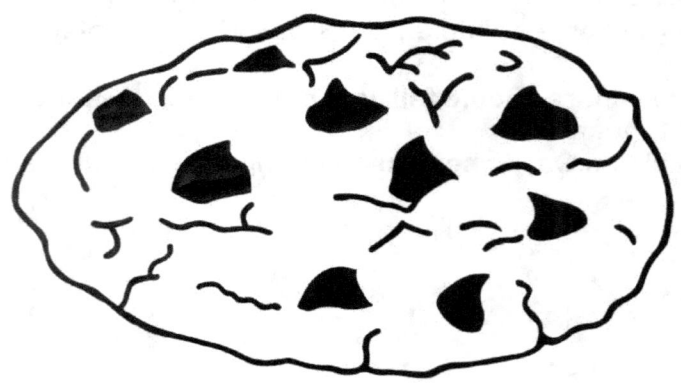

Maintaining Tolerable Compatibility

"Hi. Do you recognize me? I bought your camper van a couple years ago."
"Oh, yeah. Thanks. You saved my marriage. My wife hates camping."
"So does mine. And it saved my marriage, too. Now I can go camping alone, or just live out in the driveway during intermittent periods of banishment from the Queendom."

Your Mom Doesn't Know About This

"Grandpa, you said most things are different when you get old."
"Some things are about the same."
"What things?"
"When you're young, sometimes you think 'If my parents find out about this, they'll kill me!'"
"But your parents aren't around."
"Now sometimes I think 'If the kids find out about this, they'll kill me!'"

Something for Everyone

"The travel agent said it was the last available room within 100 miles, so we grabbed it immediately. Interesting place...rather abbreviated staff uniforms, soundproofed room, enormous hot tub and shower, mirrors over the beds. They've thought of everything... Your grandmother gets confused and wanders at night, and there were convenient handcuffs on the bedposts."

THERE MAY BE SHRINKAGE

How Long Have You Felt This Way?

"Calm down."
"I am NOT angry! I am NOT delusional!"
"OK."
"I am NOT depressed! I am NOT suicidal!"
"OK."
"I! AM! NOT! CRAZY!!!"
"OK, good. This has been a productive session, but there is something else I'd like to discuss for just a moment, if we could. My 50 minutes is almost up, Doctor."

Know Thyself

"I was skeptical after learning that a book had been written about me. How could anyone who's never even met me really know me."
"A book?"
"Well, part of one. The surprise was finding they knew me even better than I knew myself. Unfortunately, it's a book of diagnostic criteria by the American Psychiatric Association."

About That Hypothetical Glass

"Attitude is everything. Answer this, please. Do you see the glass as half empty, or as half full?"
"I wish I could just see the glass as either half empty or half full. But I can't."
"What do you see?"
"I see a conspiracy to make sure the glass is never more than half full."

Working Towards a Tolerable Consensus

"This is stupid! A complete waste of time!"
"This is the best thing you could possibly do."
"No way!"
"Don't listen to him!"
"Shut up!"
"Oh, God!"
"Hi! Thanks for coming in today. How've you been?"
"Better since that last adjustment in the medications. The voices aren't nearly so loud, argumentative, and abusive as before."

Natural Selection in Progress

"You're serious? Stop my psychiatric medications?"
"Yes, right now."
"Why? I'm doing great! Before you got me on these medications, I thought everybody was out to get me! And I was washing my hands fifty times a day! I couldn't even go to work!"
"That's exactly what you need now to survive the Coronavirus pandemic."

Not Guilty

"They're mostly executives, attorneys, politicians, cops… people who dominate, abuse, and humiliate others. They pay me to dominate, abuse, humiliate, and spank them. Do I feel guilty? Why should I?"
"Because you couldn't dominate a lapdog! Now shut up! Stop whining and bend over that couch for a real spanking!"
"But…"
"NOW!!!"
"Yes, Doctor."

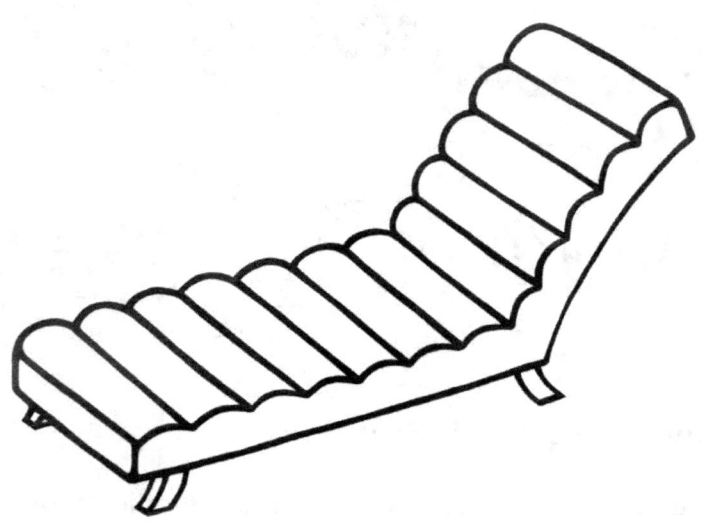

WE MET THIS REALLY WEIRD COUPLE

We're All Set Up

"Finally! I think we're all set up. It's a good thing we brought these bright flashlights. It's pitch black! The tent is up. The air mattresses are filled. The sleeping bags are ready. The cooler and the camp stove are on the table. The lawn chairs are set up. The bikes are off the bike rack. The clothesline is up. The bag with your real skimpy pink nightie is in the tent. And we've got this whole campground to ourselves. Oh, yeah! It's time to catch up on some things that we've been too busy for these last few weeks!"

"Oh, Honey! Hold me! Kiss me!"

"Oh, yeah! Oh, no! Somebody's turning into the campground. What's the chance of that happening this late on a Sunday night way out here in the middle of nowhere? Well, let's just get into bed. We've got things to do!"

"Not yet. I want to make sure they're not some weirdo creeps first."

"OK. But I'm sure they're fine. I just hope they don't make too much noise and shine bright lights over here while they're setting up."

"They're not setting up. They're not doing anything. They're just sitting in their van in the dark."

"That is kind of weird."

"Very. They're still just sitting there."

"Yeah. In the dark."

"What in the hell are they doing?"

"No idea. What if they're escaped prisoners? Or murderers? Or bank robbers on the run?"

"I don't think I'll be able to sleep tonight. And I'm keeping my clothes on, for sure."

No, I Don't Need the Light

"I think this is it. Yeah, we're finally here. I was hoping we might have the whole campground to ourselves, since it's so late on a Sunday night, but it looks like someone's in the first campsite. There are a couple more right over there. We'll take one of those. It looks like our neighbors are still up."
"Even so, it's pretty late. We should be quiet."
"Yeah. The bed is already made. All we have to do is close the curtains in the back of the van. And maybe sip some wine."
"Good idea! It's really dark. Do you need a light?"
"No, thanks. The wine, the steel cups, and the opener are all right here. I want to save our night vision so we can look at the stars."
"They were sure beautiful last night. Hey, that guy just moved his truck, put the headlights on bright, and he's pointing them right at us. What the hell!"
"So much for the night vision, but at least it'll be easier to pour. Here you go."
"Thanks. Cheers! Mmm, that's tasty."
"It sure is. Now the guy is also pointing a couple of very intense flashlights at us, just in case the headlights weren't bad enough. Am I supposed to turn the van around and aim my brights at him, too?"
"No, this is already weird enough. Let's just close the curtains, talk, sip wine, and wait him out. He'll have to turn the lights off sooner or later."
"You're right. Let's just relax. You'll love this hot spring. It's an easy twenty-minute walk from here. We'll probably have it all to ourselves if we go at dawn."
"That sounds wonderful! Then breakfast and coffee after we soak. Will you be writing while we're here?"
"Maybe, if my muse shows up. Hey, it looks like that guy finally turned all the lights off."
"Thank God! I hope these people will be easier to deal with in the daylight."

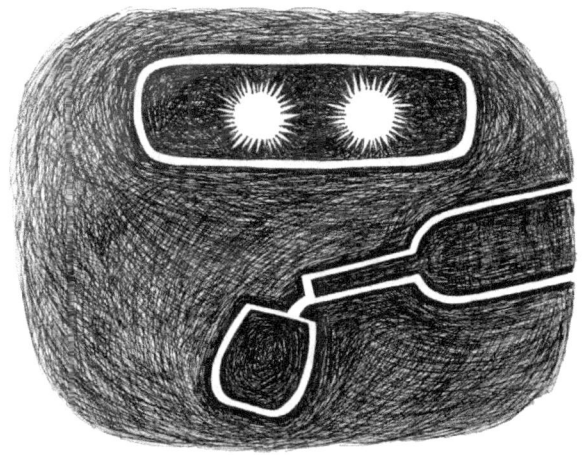

The Courier Has Arrived

"You were right! I love this place! That was a beautiful dawn walk to a wonderful hot spring. Then back here for breakfast and coffee. Does it get any better than this?"
"We'll find out soon. Our neighbors with the bright lights just got up. And it looks like they're heading this way."
"I know you're annoyed because of all the bright lights they were shining on us late last night, but, please, don't be confrontational."
"Not at all. I'm suddenly feeling very appreciative."
"Appreciative?"
"Yes. I just realized who this guy is!"
"You know this guy?"
"Sort of. He's a courier. He's come all the way out here, into the mountains, up this washboard gravel road, hours from the nearest town, to deliver my artistic license. My muse sent him."

One of the Highlights

"Good morning, neighbors. You scared the bejesus out of us last night! Coming in that late, then just sitting there in the dark like that. No tent. No trip to the restroom. Nothing! We didn't know what in the hell you were up to! We hardly slept at all!"

"Greetings, Earthlings. Do not fear. We did not require light in your visible spectrum because we retained our infrared visual capability when we transitioned to human form at the time of our arrival. And we do prefer to recalibrate our laser weaponry in darkness, which we accomplished last night."

"Huh?"

"I apologize if we caused you to experience fear, which we have read about, and especially if we have interfered with your mating behavior."

"What?"

"Whenever touring planets with oxygen rich atmospheres, we usually transform into the most intelligent species in the biosphere. However, the human mating behaviors are so entertaining that we decided on human transformation for this visit. We are certainly eager to partake in human mating behaviors!"

"You... you... what?"

"This will surely be one of the highlights of the interstellar planetary tour guide that we are preparing! And we are seeking a mating pair of humans to accompany us upon our return to Zaltar 7. Wait! Please come back! Have I said something culturally inappropriate?"

The Muse Has Poor Taste in Beer

"What an amazing week this has been!"
"Yeah! A dawn walk every morning to a world class natural hot spring. With a hot waterfall, no less! All to ourselves. And a whole campground to ourselves. Well, almost. That first night was pretty strange."
"It sure was. That couple shining the bright lights on us the first night was awfully annoying."
"True, but they left the next morning."
"I guess maybe they didn't want a free trip to Zaltar 7. You were good!"
"Thank the muse for that one."
"She was screaming at him about interstellar perverts while they were running back to their truck."
"I still feel kind of bad that they left their tent, their bikes, and everything else behind at their campsite. And that they had such terrible beer in their cooler."

THOUGHT FOR FOOD

The Gateway Vegetable

"Hot dog and fries again? Here, have a little piece of broccoli."

"No way! I've heard about that stuff! The first one's free. Then it's radishes and celery sticks. After that, it's eggplant, quinoa, spinach salads... every day, then two or three times a day. If you're not careful, you'll live to be 96! Cigarette?"

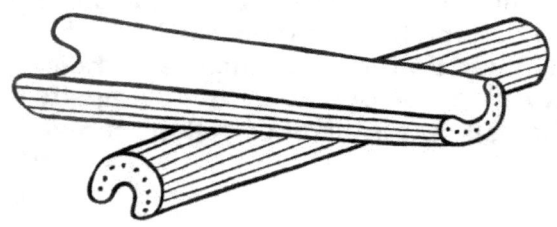

Starting Tomorrow

"I'm really glad the holidays are over. They're always fun, but hectic. And I gained so much weight!"

"Join the club."

"Me, too."

"So did I."

"Ditto. Say, these are extremely tasty. What's in them?"

"Sweet potatoes, dark chocolate, almond butter, cinnamon, maple syrup, honey..."

"I want the recipe!"

"Me, too!"

"So do I!"

"Ditto!"

THE MONTH BEFORE CHRISTMAS

'Twas the month before Christmas, and on my TV,
The stores all had specials that I just had to see.
My computer was so immeasurably worse,
So far out of control, just like some evil curse.
Making sure we don't miss any vital details,
The retailers all send us incessant emails.
Ten percent discount? Minuscule, nothing at all!
A complete waste of time! Unbelievable gall!
Expect fifty, or eighty, sometimes even more.
They'll deliver it all to your very own door.
They take MasterCard, Visa, it's never been hard,
To get ten percent more, just sign up for their card.
No payments 'til June, but they forgot to explain,
In six months your wallet will be writhing in pain.
Somehow get through Black Friday.
        Remember this fact:
You're surrounded by rudeness.
        Don't look for much tact.
If you want to succeed, and end up a winner,
You may have to act like a shark having dinner.
Dare you take a timeout the very next Sunday,
Before diving headfirst into Cyber Monday?
If you do, there's no telling just what you might miss.
Did your mom ever say it would turn out like this?
This has nothing to do with some guy in the sky,
Inexplicable urges to covet and buy.
Do you have enough closets to store all this stuff?
Is it true that enough is just never enough?
There are things in this culture so far out of whack,
That it's hard to believe
        in twelve months, they'll be back.

PESTO PIZZA CHANGED MY LIFE

Seriously Underarmed

"Can I help you find something?"
"What're you, a smart ass? Put your hands up or I'll shoot!"
"Yes, I'm a smart ass. But this is my place. And, no, I won't raise my hands. My shoulders are sore. But don't worry. I'm armed only with my wits, and my wife thinks I'm seriously underarmed. If you don't believe me, ask her. Here she is now."
"My husband is seriously underarmed. I, however, am seriously armed. Any move you make will be your last."

The Situation

"Let me explain the situation to you, just to make sure you understand. I am pointing a pistol at your husband, at very close range. If you do not do as I say, right now, I will kill your husband. Do you understand the situation?"
"I do. So I will explain it to you, to make sure that you understand. You are pointing a pistol at my husband, not at me. I am pointing a pistol, also at close range, at you. If you do not kill my husband, right now, I will kill you."

You Two May Have Things to Discuss

"Let me explain the situation to you. You're pointing a pistol at me. My wife is pointing a pistol at you. She's told you that if you do not kill me, she will kill you. She hasn't mentioned that I've installed a security camera system with an internet connection and recording."
"I disconnected the camera! Shoot him!"
"She disconnected one camera. I see that you're now pointing your pistols at each other. This is becoming interesting, but, unfortunately, I've got a prior commitment. So, if you'll excuse me, I'm signed up for a poker tournament."

We May Have Trust Issues

"I'm really sorry your husband just left you here alone like this. What if something went wrong?"
"I guess he's not worried about me."
"You have such a commanding presence!"
"Why, thank you! How about you? Are you married?"
"Not for much longer. And she's trying to take absolutely everything."
"I'm sorry. You're so open and communicative! So daring, yet vulnerable."
"I wish you and I had met under different circumstances."
"Yes, I'd love to get to know you better."
"That might be easier if we weren't pointing these pistols at each other."

Pesto Pizza and Zinfandel

"You two haven't budged an inch since I left five hours ago."
"How much did you lose at the poker tournament?"
"I did really well!"
"How much did we win?"
"Plenty! And I picked up a large pesto pizza and a bottle of Zinfandel."
"It smells wonderful!"
"It's to die for! Sorry, poor choice of words. The Zin is jammy, peppery. Aren't you going to have some?"
"Maybe later."
"OK. I'm going out again. I'll leave the pizza and wine right here. You two can help yourselves when you're done pointing your pistols at each other."

The Best Part of the Whole Day!

"That pizza was incredible! Pesto and chicken?
That's your favorite?"
"Yes, with sun dried tomatoes and caramelized
onions. But the best part of the whole day was you!
I've never had such intimate conversations with
anyone before! I feel like I've known you my whole
life!"
"Agreed. And you're awesome! So calm and
confident under pressure!"
"No way! I was sweating like crazy!"
"This has been the weirdest, most intense, what?
First date?"
"It's amazing what can happen when two complete
strangers unexpectedly spend that many hours
pointing pistols at each other. You'll call, right?"

TWO HALVES

This Snuck up on Me

"Thanks for such a wonderful time. I've really enjoyed myself tonight."
"I have, too. I'd love to see you again. Walking along the river was beautiful. And that wine was amazing!"
"That wine waited twelve years for this moment."
"That's a long time."
"I feel like I've waited all my life for this moment."

Just a Coincidence

"Do you still have great grandma's wedding dress?"
"Yes, and it's a beautiful dress, but that may not be a good idea."
"Why not?"
"Your great grandmother, your grandmother, and I all wore it, and we were all widows by age 30."
"He's been kind of a jerk lately. I'd like to try it on."

Comprehension Limited by Genetic Factors

"OK, I'm ready... What's the matter? Why are you looking at me like that? What?"
"You're not really planning to wear that? Are you? Really?"
"Well, yeah, sure, I..."
"No."
"Huh?"
"You are not doing this to me! Not tonight!"
"I... uh... uh... I'll be right back."

But for a Perfectly Good Reason

"We're late again. You're so pokey!"

"Everyone will understand. I've got a perfectly good reason."

"What's your excuse this time?"

"It's not an excuse! I was in the cellar mulling over the wine selection, to make sure I'd pick the perfect bottle for this evening."

"Are you forgetting that people will be tasting it? And that someone may even look at the label?"

"Right, right. OK... We had to drop our beloved pet goldfish off at the emergency veterinary aquarium ICU."

"You used that last time."

"I did? Well, then, I was so engrossed in my online Amish televangelist course that..."

"No. Even our host wouldn't believe that one."

"So, let's see... Of course! I had to stop off for an emergency cash transfer. I got a call from a sort of investment counselor. Interesting guy, a Nigerian prince, actually, in a bit of an awkward position, it seems. He's due to come into an incredibly large amount of money soon, but, unfortunately, he's kind of short at the moment, and in need of a sizable short-term loan. Any cash that I can wire to him immediately, will later be repaid ten times over."

"No one will believe that you fell for that!"

"Of course not. You see, although I wanted to help out, I couldn't. After the house burned down, the insurance company screwed me so badly that I was living in a refrigerator box under a bridge, until that got stolen while I was in the hospital for heart surgery. Lately, I've been trying to figure out how best to get arrested so that I can get out of the weather and have a few tolerable meals. There was a lot more, but he cut me off and offered to send me an emergency cash transfer. So, we're a little late."

Here We Are

"Turn left here."
"OK. I think we're almost there."
"Yeah. Turn right at the next street."
"I think it's about halfway down... this is it. We're here. This'll be fun."
"It should be, but..."
"But what?"
"Could you try to be just a little bit less 'you' tonight?"

Just One Quick Stop

"Well, that was fun."
"I'm glad you enjoyed it. Say, would you mind if we made just one quick stop on the way home?"
"OK, I guess. But it's late and we've had quite a bit to drink. What could you possibly need right now that can't wait until tomorrow?"
"A bottle of wine and some rat poison."

Saving It for Marriage

"Oh, come on!"
"No! We're not married!"
"'It's been three weeks!"
"Too bad! Three weeks ago, after 62 years of marriage, you insisted that we get a divorce, because you said I was trying to control you. So, we got divorced."
"OK. Will you marry me? Again?"
"Yes."
"So, now..."
"Not until our honeymoon."

Here's Why You Need Me

"I was very pleasantly surprised when you agreed to go out with me the first time."

"You were charming, and a great dancer."

"And you kissed me, with unexpected intensity, even after learning that I had something important in common with your first husband."

"But not the psychiatric or substance abuse issues. You also had a lot of other things going for you. And essentially nothing in common with my second husband. When we went out the next time, you still kept your hands to yourself. No pressure. I liked that, too."

"But when we kissed goodbye after our third date, it really felt like goodbye. So, I was surprised at your response when I texted you a week later to ask if you'd started on your road trip yet. You suggested that we take a walk before you left later that day."

"I realized that you were actually listening to me. That got my attention. During that walk, I learned that you're also somewhat trainable."

"Those things are nice, but here's why you really need me in your life. We've each survived two disastrous marriages. Each of our former spouses had at least two or three major psychiatric, emotional, or substance abuse issues that made permanent close interpersonal relationships virtually impossible. Nonetheless, you hold yourself at least partly responsible for both terrible marriages."

"True. So what?"

"So, no matter how much of a calamity you feel you've made of your life, it'll help if you're able to look at me."

"So that I can have your shining example of perfection to guide me?"

"Quite the contrary. Because when you look at the total wreck that I've made of my personal life, you'll be reminded that maybe you haven't messed things up as badly as you thought you had."

We're Not Children!

"When they find out we're seeing each other..."
"They did everything they could to break us up before."
"And it worked."
"For awhile."
"They have no right to control us!"
"They'll say they don't want us to get hurt."
"Maybe we should elope."
"Again? We're not children!"
"No. They are. Ours, in fact."

Miranda

"How come it's always about my screaming?!?! How come it's never about you being such a jerk?!?! And it's even worse since you got that promotion!!! Mr Big Shot Detective!!! What're you going to do, arrest me for disturbing the peace?!?!"
"No, but I will advise you that you have the right to remain silent."

Let's Talk About Next Week Now

"I'll be home around six. Is there anything I should pick up?"
"Yeah. I'll order a couple pizzas."
"A couple? Are we having company?"
"I invited your ex."
"Again? We just did that!"
"That was your other ex."
"Why are you doing this?"
"After you see them, you always appreciate me a lot more.

Porno Update

"I'd love to, but I've got to go straight home and get my husband into the sack. He's been texting me some very arousing photos!"
"Your husband of 30 years is texting you porno?"
"Look at these. He had the day off and did the laundry, cleaned the bathrooms, the kitchen, vacuumed..."
"Oh! Oh!! Oh!!!"

The Best Birthday Ever

"Thank you for the best birthday ever! Dinner, roses, and wine! I love you."
"And I love you. Now I'll give you anything you want. And I mean anything."
"Well, I've had this fantasy..."
"I'm your sex slave for the night."
"...a hot, sexy guy, completely naked..."
"I'm your guy."
"...cleaning the bathroom."

Priorities

"Help me out here... We don't know yet when we can schedule Tammy's wedding, your gallbladder surgery, our flights to Europe, the signing tour for my new book, Mom's memorial service, remodel the kitchen, list the house, or trade in the car, because we're waiting to hear from your hairdresser?"
"Maybe we'll hear next week."

Do I Know You?

"Sorry I can't take your call right now. Please leave a message and I'll call back just as soon as I can."
"Honey, it's me again, for the 25th time. Are you OK? Please call. I saw in the paper that the lottery ticket we bought won $58,000,000!! Did you see that?"

Like Pulling Teeth

"Good morning. How are you today?"
"Fine."
"Honey, tell the doctor what's wrong! He can't help you if he doesn't know what's wrong with you!"
"Let's try this again. What's wrong?"
"Ask her."
"No way! If I started asking women what's wrong with their husbands, I'd be here 'til midnight every night. Now what's wrong?"

PRAGMATISM

Yeah, Him

"What do you think? Should we have a New Year's
Eve party again this year?"
"Maybe, depending on who we invite. There was one
guy last year who got pretty drunk and obnoxious. I
don't want him to come."
"Then we won't invite him."
"OK. So, for New Year's Eve, you'll go visit your
sister?"

Let Me Think This Over

"Hello."
"Hi! How are you?"
"Kind of annoyed. Some jerk is trying to steal my
identity. I've had to talk with three credit card
companies and the post office. Anyway, what would
you like to do Friday night?"
"That depends. How much of your identity is this guy
stealing? And what does he look like?"

The Hyphen's Not the Issue

"Sometimes she used her name, sometimes my name,
sometimes her name, hyphen, my name. I told her I
didn't care either way, but said I would like to know
who I'd married."
"So what happened?"
"Sometimes, even after all these years, we're both
still trying to figure out just who each of us actually
married."

They Laughed Later

"You ran that stop sign, sir. I'll need to see your driver's license and the vehicle registration."
"You write him a ticket! He could have killed somebody!"
"Is this your wife?"
"How could you tell?"
"I'll let you off with a warning this time. You've got enough trouble already. Stop for the stop signs, OK?"

Not a Dry Eye

"Did that prescription help your dry eyes?"
"It burned them, but they're OK without medication since I started watching chick flicks with my wife every night. They're moist because the movies make me cry. We're also talking more, and we never argue anymore."
"No arguments! Could you write down a few movie titles for me?"

You'll Get Used to It

"This pandemic has been going on for months, and I still don't get this whole social distancing thing. Stay far away from people! Don't touch! It's driving me crazy!"
"I'm used to it."
"From your work at the hospital?"
"No. Because for the last five years that's how I've had to interact with my wife."

OF COURSE IT MAKES SENSE

It's Not About You! Really!

"Every other online reviewer gave my short story collection five stars. You gave it one, and said it sucked. Earlier you said you loved every story!"
"Not the one about the woman who threw her bathroom scale out the 12th floor window!"
"Honey, it's time we kissed and made up."
"Explain that to your attorney."

Pseudo Polygamy

"It must be what? 30 years?"
"At least."
"Still popular with the women?"
"I'm very close to what seems like several of them."
"Several! Are you crazy?"
"It's not what it sounds like! It's really just one woman, but with her moods, it sometimes seems like there are several of them."

Staying Busy

"Are you married?"
"Twice. Not currently."
"You should do it again."
"Our relationship is fantastic right now. Why ruin it? How about you?"
"We combined families three years ago, but never married. Do you think we should?"
"Making my own mistakes is a full-time job. I don't have time to help make yours, too."

We Do the Best We Can

"How long have you two been married?"
"We've been together for several years, but we're not married. We've each had a couple of disastrous previous marriages."
"So you're living together in sin?"
"No, we live apart. But, when we have time, we do try to live apart together as sinfully as possible."

A Bit of an Upgrade

"Superhero Super Costumes. How may I help you?"
"You can start by explaining this $20,000 charge on my credit card statement."
"That's our standard deposit. Our indestructible costumes can withstand just about anything. You must understand that the latest materials and the special processing required do come at some expense. Let me see... Our only recent order came in a week ago. Form fitting, of course, built over a wax model torso, with a graphic of three Z's on the chest."
"I sleep through alarm clocks, and even through my husband's snoring. He says that's my superpower, and calls me Slumber Woman. When I went to bed the other night, he was shopping for flannel pajamas for me. He was going to have "ZZZ" embroidered on the chest. When I woke up in the morning, there was an empty wine bottle near his laptop."

The Ultimate Relationship

"I didn't think I'd ever feel like this again!"
"My feelings for you snuck up on me, too. We just met last week, but we've already become a couple!"
"We're both in our 90's, so long range plans are out."
"Then let's just think of it as a summer fling."

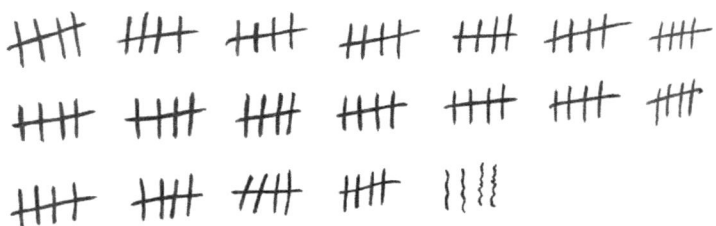

Comprehensive Wedding Planning

"Daily News. Advertising. How can I help you?"
"I'd like some space in the upcoming annual Bridal Section."
"Of course. What will we be advertising?"
"This is Saul Cupid. I practice family law, specializing in prenuptial agreements and divorce."
"That may be awkward in the annual Bridal Section."
"The Gazette had no problem. But if..."
"Really?"
"Really. The file is already set up."
"Well, OK, I guess. Can you email it to me?"
"Will do. Thanks. Bye."
"Bye."
...
"Gazette. Advertising. How can I help you?"
"I'd like some space in the upcoming annual Bridal Section."

YOU WERE EXPECTING WHAT?

Pandemic Salvation

Stores not deemed essential were told to close up
      shop.
Stay home if you can. Let the daily death count
      drop.
Some religious businessmen, ecclesiastic,
Still hold on-site meetings, serving hope fantastic.
Is their main concern to honor resurrection?
Could it be salvation of the church collection?

```
              $$$$$$$$
              $$$$$$$$
              $$$$$$$$
              $$$$$$$$
$$$$$$$$$$$$$$$$$$$$$$$$$$$$$
$$$$$$$$$$$$$$$$$$$$$$$$$$$$$
$$$$$$$$$$$$$$$$$$$$$$$$$$$$$
$$$$$$$$$$$$$$$$$$$$$$$$$$$$$
              $$$$$$$$
              $$$$$$$$
              $$$$$$$$
              $$$$$$$$
              $$$$$$$$
              $$$$$$$$
              $$$$$$$$
              $$$$$$$$
              $$$$$$$$
              $$$$$$$$
```

Two's Company

"So, you told her you really liked her a lot."
"Right. Then she said she wouldn't enter into an
intimate relationship unless there were three of us.
She said that from our earlier conversations, she
didn't think I'd be into that scene."
"A threesome! With one of her friends?"
"Yeah. Her, and me, and Jesus."

She Prays for Him Every Night

"And finally, dear Lord, I pray, as I pray every night, for the most evil man I've ever met. As always, I pray that you will make him a better man immediately. And if, in your infinite wisdom, you decide that the only way to make him a better man is for him to leave this world, and pass into the next, so be it. If so, please remember that this man sees himself as equal to your only begotten son, and will, therefore, only embrace a departure involving truly biblical amounts of suffering. Amen."

They're Favored This Time

"I've booked Dad's trip with Time Travel Tours. Reservations were tight, because time travel is still so new. The only date available was Thanksgiving."
"Oh, no! He's cheered for the Detroit Lions every Thanksgiving for decades!"
"It'll be OK. He'll be in the Roman Coliseum 2,000 years ago. He can still cheer for the lions."

The Embrace

"I've decided to accept your God."
"Wonderful! Was it my teaching?"
"Somewhat... mostly your actions."
"I'm embarrassed, but, please, explain."
"You have taught that there is a just God."
"Yes!"
"And Heaven, and Satan, and Hell. So, if I embrace your just God, then I can believe that you will spend all eternity in Hell."

IN THE PUDDING

Non-Conversion Therapy

"Hello."

"Hi! My name's..."

"What're you selling?"

"I'm not selling anything."

"Then why'd you knock on my door?"

"I'm trying to talk to everyone and leave them a pamphlet and an invitation to our..."

"You're selling eternal salvation."

"That's not for sale."

"Because it doesn't exist. But that won't stop you from trying."

"There's no charge for..."

"The upfront costs include attendance and suspension of rational skepticism. Financial transactions come later, along with brand-specific rituals, abstinences, product logos, and a rewards club."

"This is based on ancient, sacred writings by first hand witnesses of actual events."

"Each with unknown accuracy and intent, later subjected to generations of translators of potentially questionable veracity and ability. You can't even believe the news that's reported today, and you believe this?"

"But God..."

"A lot of gods have come and gone. Do you believe in Zeus?"

"Of course not! But God..."

"Which one?"

"The only one."

"There are several up and running right now. But yours is the only real one. Don't be fooled by cheap imitations! Call the number on your screen before midnight tonight! Operators are standing by! Could

you treat others well without a god?"
"I don't think..."
"Could you justify war without a god?"
"You're making me think about..."
"About how you can save this poor sinner who's strayed from the path of righteousness?"
"About my own beliefs. Do you have a pamphlet that I could take with me?"
"Sure. Here you are. Thanks for coming by."

Amen!

"Come on, let's just eat."
"No. I want someone to say grace."
"OK, I'll do it. Dear God, if there really is one, thank you for this wonderful meal. And if there really are more than one of you, would you please get your followers to stop killing each other in your names? Amen."
"Amen!"

Just for the Hell of It

"Classic or custom?"
"Is classic really hellfire and brimstone?"
"Yes, with pitchforks."
"What's custom like?"
"How about spending eternity with your ex-wife?"
"OK. She's annoying, but I always enjoyed slapping her around. Maybe Hell won't be so bad!"
"Sign here, in blood.... very good. Oh, I almost forgot! She's a martial arts instructor now."

PALPABLE STORIES

OK, OK, OK

"Get up!"
"Huh?"
"Get me out of here!"
"It's 5 AM! I was up late. You're just a block of marble!"
"To everyone else I'm just a block of marble. But you know I'm in here! You know my every curve, angle, and texture. I'll be the best sculpture you've ever done! Now get up!"

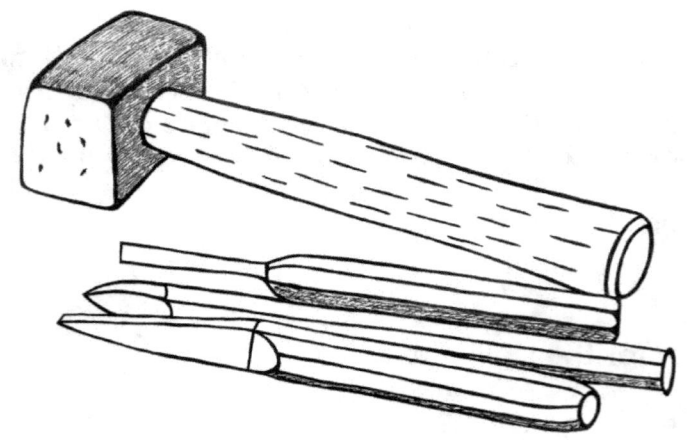

The Learning Curve

"I love your work. How'd you get started?"
"I started with inexpensive tools and materials, and, at first, agonized slowly and timidly over every little mistake. As I gained experience, I was able to get better tools and better materials. That gave me the confidence and efficiency to make bigger, better, and more interesting mistakes."

DON'T THINK ABOUT IT TOO MUCH, OK?

Focused Intervention

"Excuse me. I have to unplug a drain. Could you please... what're you doing here? In that vest? Are you working here?"

"Part time. Today's my last day."

"How do you even have time? Every psychiatrist in our group practice, including you, is working 10-hour days, and we're all booked solid for six months. Isn't that stressful enough for you?"

"I thought this would be less stressful, so I thought I'd give it a try. But now, instead of seeing 10 or 15 people with mental health issues every day, I see 60 or 70. So I'm quitting. What about that plugged drain?"

"Oh, yeah. It took eight years to finally get my wife to move here, away from her mother. Talk about multiple psychiatric diagnoses! And now her mother has moved here! Her kitchen sink is plugged, but that's the least of that woman's problems, let me tell you!"

"No! Please don't! Plumbing is on Aisle 14."

The Omertà

"I've been watching you. I like the way you handle yourself. I was talking with the Don..."

"About me?"

"Yeah. We think you're ready to move up. But remember that he's very big on absolute loyalty and the omertà."

"The code of silence. Talk and you're dead."

"Right."

"What's he got in mind?"

"Attorney General."

To Do List Monday

Tweet - voting hoax
And Friends
Tweet - virus hoax
Hair
Make up
Briefing - boring!
Mickey D!
Presser - I'm doing a great job, it's going away,
        hydroxychloroquine, tell reporter she's stupid
Tweet - fake news
Tweet - fire somebody
Bucket!
Executive Order - showerheads
Bean photo
Tweet - doing great job
Whoppers!
Tucker
Tweet - law and order
Call Sean
Laura

I Probably Did Her a Favor

"Whatever... Like, how was I supposed to know what
she was going to do? And she was, like, ancient, sixty
or something. So, who even cares? I probably did
her a favor. And everyone, I mean everyone, was
posting shots of their new haircuts, like, every few
seconds. Then everyone else was posting their
comments. And my hair is just so last month, you
know? And all my calls to my hairdresser were going
to voicemail."
"Counselor, you will inform your client that 'whatever'
is not an acceptable plea for a charge of vehicular
homicide."

This Is So Cool!

"Hello."
"Good morning! We're from…"
"Ooh! Hold it! Time out! Let me grab my phone. I want to film this. OK. Thanks! This is so cool! I'm doing my thesis on religious cults, and…"
"We're not a cult! We're a legitimate…"
"Sorry. Of course. I forgot. Self-identification as a cult is a no-no. Anyway, I'm glad I just happened to be home right now, or I'd have missed you. And my advisor will be so excited! Let's see, I want to ask about virgin sacrifice. I mean, not death, not anymore, just sexually, right? Is it, like, just the clergy, or…"
"That is extremely offensive!"
"Oh, uh, excuse me. I didn't mean… uh, well, how about special rituals, speaking in tongues, or, uh, special, uh, clothing, or…. Wait! Come back!"

We'd Love To!

"Yes! We'd love to! Hold on… Mary! Can you check Matthew's diaper? Thanks. Sorry. Yes, Thursday nights would be fine. Just a sec… Mark! You and Luke and John and Paul go outside! Now! What was I… Oh, yeah, I'm so glad you asked! Timothy will be delighted, too. Hold on… Frances, will you give Joseph his bottle? Thanks. I'm back. Timothy just started a third job, but he's free on Thursday nights. Excuse me…. David, will you please help Samuel and James with their arithmetic? Thank you. Let's see… Hold it… Eve, would you check on Bartholomew and Thaddeus? Thanks. Yes, Reverend, we'll… just a minute…. Rebecca, would you see if Michael needs to go potty? And give Philip a cookie? Thanks. Sorry… Yes, we'd love to talk with the premarital counseling group about natural birth control."

The Gazette-Journal

"Hello?"
"Hi! I'm calling to tell you about great new subscription rates for the Gazette-Journal!"
"Oooooooh ... Do they still have stories about murders, rapes and drive-by shootings?"
"Well, yes, sometimes, but ..."
"How about earthquakes and fires?"
"Well, yes, but ..."
"And bombings! Plane crashes!! Executions! Tidal waves! Wars! Plagues! Starvation! Suicide! Impalement! Electrocution!!!
"Good night, sir."
Click.

Times Have Changed

"It's just not done like that anymore. Times have changed."
"It's not fair! My great grandpa used to lynch them. My grandpa burned crosses in their yards, and took my dad when he was just a kid."
"OK, I'll call my fishing buddy. He's in charge of hiring for the Sheriff."

A Place to Rest

"We all know these are uncertain times. Are you prepared for the loss of loved ones? Do you have enough memorial urns for your family? Buy two urns now and get a third free! This offer ends at midnight tonight! While supplies last! Call the number on your screen now! Operators are standing by!"

WHOSE FAMILY?

Pineapples and Walnuts

"Don't get me wrong. I love them to death, but now I remember why we haven't seen them for ten years."
"No kidding. We could not possibly be any further apart from them if we tried. They're not stupid. I know they're not. But I'll never understand how they could believe and say so many stupid things! At first it seems like they've got to be joking, you know?"
"I know. I'm glad you thought to set up a signal word in advance, so we could let each other know when it was time to call for the check and get out of there before they drove us crazy."
"Yeah, me too. But I was starting to think you'd forgotten all about it. I mentioned Hawaiian pizza with pineapple, nothing. Then pineapple upside down cake, and then Pineapple Express. After I brought up pineapple smoothies the second time, you finally seemed to get it. I was about to explode! I was afraid they might wonder why I kept using that same word over and over."
"Sorry. Don't worry, they'd never figure that out. I actually got it the first time, but became interested in the conversation. I didn't know they had a walnut tree in their yard, or that she was making banana walnut bread and walnut ice cream. And he's been making furniture. It sounds beautiful! A walnut table, walnut chairs, with matching walnut coasters and walnut napkin rings."
"Yeah, what's with all the walnut stuff?"
"I don't know. But don't worry about the pineapple thing. They'd never figure that out."

Now Tell Me the Truth

"No! You can't use it!"

"But it's just a drawing of a hand holding a plate!"

"It's not just a drawing of a hand holding a plate. It's a drawing of my hand holding a plate."

"No one will ever know it's your hand!"

"I'll know."

"Come on! You know how long it took me to do that drawing!"

"Well, you should have told me how it looked."

"It looks fine! Come on! I need this. Help me out. Please."

"Only if we start over with another plate."

"This is ridiculous!"

"Take it or leave it."

"OK. Here. How about this plate?"

"Maybe. Now tell me the truth. Does this plate make me look fat?"

No Ifs, Ands, or Buts

"You've come to this morning's press conference! I know we don't always see eye to eye. I'll be announcing a major project."

"I know. I can't really stay. I just came to remind you that I'll always love you. Gotta run."

"And I'll always love you. Organizing another protest?"

"Yes."

"Where's this one?"

"Just outside."

I Mean It!

"Mom! Mom!"
"What is it this time?"
"He put his stuff on my half of the table! Again!"
"I said I'm sorry."
"And he's humming! Again!"
"I am not."
"He is, too! Make him stop!"
"Listen to me! Both of you! If you don't stop this, right now, I'm moving back to Assisted Living!"

A Little Change in Plans

"Your wedding's coming up in just three months.
I still haven't booked my flights. When should
I arrive? Will I be walking you down the aisle?"
"No, we've changed our plans. We were originally
going to invite 200 people, but decided to cut back a
little bit."
"Oh. How many will you be inviting?"
"199."

Everything?

"Everything in moderation! I've told you that since
you were born!"
"You've said it thousands of times. Consider this. If
you have everything in moderation, everything, then
you have to have moderation in moderation. You
can't have moderation in moderation without having
some extremes."
"I'll help you if you decide to go to law school."

WORKING ON RELATIONSHIPS

Potential

"I was worried at first, but you two really hit it off!
How'd that happen?"
"After we talked a bit, I think she decided that I had
potential."
"Potential for what?"
"You suggested that she'd been the family nut case
for years. I think she decided that maybe I could take
over in that capacity."

No Surprises Here

"How was the memorial service? I'm sorry I couldn't
go."
"You would've loved it! Everybody reconnected with
everybody! Aunts, uncles, cousins, nieces,
nephews... fantastic! And nobody went on and on
about getting into Heaven, or spending eternity with
God, nothing like that. Of course, it being Uncle Jack,
there was some mention of Hell."

It's Just for the Weekend

"I don't wanna stay with her! She's mean to me!"
"It's just for the weekend, Honey. I really need for you
to do this. She said she'll order pizza. You can watch
any movies you want. Please, Honey, I really need
this weekend."
"If I wanted to stay with her, I wouldn't have divorced
her."

Only the Names Have Been Changed

"Another family disagreement?"
"Yes, and we need Mom to talk with Uncle Gil. I talked with Jack. He'll try to get Uncle Gil to agree to talk with Mom."
"And?"
"Would you try to get Cobb to get Mom to talk with me? I'll try to get her to agree to talk with Uncle Gil."

Family Ties

Dear Dad,

Never thought I'd find you! Mom just knew there was a sperm donor somewhere. Then I connected with your cousin through the genetic testing service. I'm coming to see you! We don't have to talk about those 37 people at the mall, or about Death Row. I just want to meet my dad!

There Will Be Unannounced Quizzes

"It's so nice to finally meet you! He's told me so much about you."
"We met five years ago this week."
"Wonderful! He said you teach at the college?"
"No, I don't teach. I'm administrative faculty. Although I guess I have been trying to teach behavior for the last five years."

GETTING TO KNOW YOU

Desirability and Charm

"Thanks for inviting me to dinner."
"I'm glad you could come."
"I brought a couple bottles of wine."
"Thanks, but I'm sure one will be plenty."
"I agree, but I thought you'd like a choice."
"You mean for the best food and wine pairing?"
"That's one approach, but sometimes other considerations may be even more important."
"Like what?"
"One of these is pretty young, so if we don't finish the whole bottle, whatever is left will still be good tomorrow."
"And the other?"
"It's mature, at the peak of it's desirability and charm. But it would be a shame not to finish the bottle, because anything left for tomorrow wouldn't be nearly as good. And, by the time we finish the bottle, you may also find me to be at the peak of my desirability and charm."
"That settles it! Desirability and charm!"

Motivation

"A group of us just get together, read a play, and drink wine. We never know beforehand what play or what part..."
"No chance to prepare? I'd want time to understand my character's motivation."
"My characters always have the same motivation."
"What?"
"To read well enough that they get to have another glass of wine."

To My New Neighbors Across the Street

These are strange times. I've been away from home a lot the last couple months. I assume that you're the guy who sprayed herbicide along the curb in front of my house. If so, please never do that again. Some herbicides are toxic, carcinogenic poisons. The stuff will almost certainly find its way into the walnuts that grow on the tree in my yard, which was, until a few days ago, organically grown. Usually, nobody wants to poison me unless I'm married to them. Again, these are strange times.

The Guy Across the Street

To My New Neighbors, Again

Sorry. Bad assumption on my part. Another neighbor has informed me that the city sprayed the herbicide in front of my house, not you. He has also informed me that I'm not an idiot all the time, just often enough that I should familiarize myself with the concept.
Again, sorry.

The Guy Across the Street

I've Got This Covered

"I think your homeowners and auto policies will be OK with these upgrades. We should also discuss long term care insurance."
"I won't need it. You've read some of my writing, and heard about some of the practical jokes I've played. You've had enough conversations with me to know. Someday, somebody will surely murder me."

We Interrupt This Fiction...

"I already told you!"

"I didn't ask you about that. I can't ask you about that. I can't even write that down. Let's back up. Your doctors are excellent, and they'll be working hard to get you all better as soon as possible. I'm a social worker with the hospital. Occasionally I have to call a member of the clergy. That's the only reason I asked you about your religion."

"How many times do I..."

"You didn't give me the name of a religion. You gave me the name of a political party."

"That's my religion!"

Only Twelve Steps?

"My name is Susan. I'm ad... I'm addict... I can't say it!"

"Every person in this room has been where you are now. The first step is to admit you have a problem. Sorry, poor choice of words."

"I can stop any time I want!"

"Do you realize that you're stepping in place right now?"

Thanks for Calling

"I always thought it was, like, really stupid when I saw other kids holding hands, and kissing. But all summer, with you... It felt... It felt weird, but really good. Then your family moved last week, and..."

"Yeah. Listen, thanks for calling. I met this guy at my new school..."

ENERGIZED

Evening Workout

"Hi. This is a surprise. Come on in. What are you up to?"

"I just felt like I needed to run, and ended up here."

"OK. Here, have a drink. You know there's a curfew in effect because of the protests, right? It was on the news. The police are wearing riot gear, gassing, clubbing, and arresting protesters. And you decided to go out for a run?"

"I just felt like I really needed to run. I wasn't the only one. There was another guy running with me part of the way, too. I've been running for an hour or two every day, but usually alone. It's different, running with a partner. Sometimes each of us tries to spur the other on to do their very best. This guy was really working hard, huffing and puffing. Every time he'd slow down, I'd slow down a little bit, too, and let him almost catch up. That seemed to prod him to pick up the pace himself. Then I'd speed up again. We did that several times. It made for a pretty decent workout."

"I'm sure he appreciated that."

"I'm not so sure. He finally stopped and sat down on the ground. He was completely covered with sweat, and his face was extremely red. I stopped, too, and made what I thought was a helpful suggestion. He was gasping for breath and couldn't even talk, but the look on his face gave me the impression that I may have triggered some very negative feelings on his part. It seemed like he might need some time alone to work through those feelings, so I left him there."

"What did you suggest?"

"I suggested that maybe the next time he goes running he shouldn't wear all that riot gear."

Presentation Preparation

"Next."
"Coffee, please."
"This is obviously your first time here. We serve espresso, some single origin, mostly blended. What're you up to this morning?"
"I'm doing a budget presentation at a committee meeting in an hour."
"In this recession? I'll pull a double shot of our Body Armor Blend. Step to the register, please. Next."

Unprecedented Optimism

"Hi! How's your morning going?"
"We just now decided to get married!"
"Congratulations! I'll pull a couple shots of our Unprecedented Optimism Espresso Blend, on the house."
"We've already seen the menu. I'd like a shot of the Pregnant Pause Blend, please."
"OK. And you?"
"I'd like a triple shot of the Sweating Bullets Blend."

Today's the Day

"Hi! Welcome to Espresso for All! How's your morning going?"
"I've got to get my husband to clean the garage. He keeps procrastinating."
"Maybe you'd like our Gentle Persuasion Blend. It's a complex medium roast blend from Sumatra, Peru, and Kona. Unbelievable finish!"
"Not this time. I'll have a quad shot of the Intimidating Dominatrix."

A MATTER OF PERSPECTIVE

Fast Forward Fifty Years

"I told you that your offer was so low as to be considered antagonistic and offensive, and I told you why. I suggested an offer that I felt was more reasonable, and that I felt would almost certainly have been accepted. You insisted on the lower offer. Now, the counteroffer is..."

"This is robbery!"

"If we don't come up with a reasonable settlement very soon, you'll find out about robbery. The counteroffer isn't that bad. It might be reasonable to come in a little bit lower, but not much, not now."

"No way! We'll take them to court if we have to!"

"Let me tell you about a settlement I was involved in, as one of two litigants, fifty years ago, in the Court of Mom. We were five and six years old. There was one cookie left."

"You expect me to pay your hourly rate while you tell me about a fifty year-old argument over a cookie!"

"I'm trying to save you a lot of aggravation, time, and money. So calm down."

"Our mom broke it in two. Each of us felt the other had the bigger half, but there was no pleasing us. Neither of us was willing to swap halves, or come to any other reasonable agreement. Mom got sick of our squabbling. She ate both halves herself, right in front of us, one bite at a time. She told us how good it was the whole time. If you don't settle this case, very soon, you'll find yourself in the same situation I found myself in fifty years ago. But it'll cost you a lot more than half a cookie to learn now what I learned then."

The Eye of the Beholder

"How was the opening? Anything interesting?"
"There was an unusual sculpture, called The Eye of the Beholder."
"Unusual how?"
"There were male and female nude figures standing in front of full-length mirrors. She looked young, slender, shapely, and attractive, brushing her hair before the mirror. But the image looking back at her from the mirror was old, saggy, wrinkled, and very obese."
"Too many women feel that way about themselves. How about him?"
"Just the opposite. The figure giving himself a shave in front of the mirror was balding, wrinkled, saggy, and had a belly large enough to conceal anything else that might be considered obscene. But the image looking back from the mirror was young, lean, and muscular, with a full head of hair and a six-pack abdomen. Below the waist, he rather resembled a horse."
"Ah, yes, a work of Modern Delusional Realism."

Rough Draft

"You got published! Frankly, I liked some of your other stories more than this one."
"I think the paper selected for this particular manuscript was crucial."
"Why?"
"The editor told me to submit as many stories as I liked, said he'd use whatever he didn't publish for personal hygiene."
"So?"
"This one was on sandpaper."

THAT'S ONE WAY TO LOOK AT IT

An Absolute Genius

"... his comments today in the Rose Garden."
"It's a great virus, the best virus, really. It's a perfect virus! And we're using it to fix Social Security. We're fixing Social Security! By cutting down recipients. Not too many deaths, really. And we're doing a great job."
"An absolute genius! We'll return after these messages."

Quite the Contrary

"Excuse me, sir. Smoking is not permitted in the building."
"Oh, you're one of them, huh? You probably don't like abortion, either, do you?"
"I don't feel that way at all. I think it's a shame there hasn't been at least one more abortion."
"One more?"
"Yes. It's too bad your mother didn't have one."

Change of Shift

"The patient in 716 has a complex groin wound. Three female RN's have done the dressing change every shift, one for the dressing, and two to spread her legs. You'll do it alone."
"Why?"
"Because we're short-staffed, and you've bragged that every woman in the world wants to spread her legs for you."

It's Personal

"Hi! This is a surprise! Come in. How are you?"
"I was fine until I started reading this book of short stories you wrote! Especially this one you wrote about me! It's so embarrassing!"
"Which one?"
"It's on page... this one."
"Thanks. A lot of people thought that was about them! And nobody was happy."

Just a Little

"I've heard that you roast your own coffee."
"I do. Occasionally on Saturday mornings I have coffee parties."
"That sounds like fun."
"It is, although one friend says the people who come are so smart that she's a little intimidated. I told her I'd dumb it down a bit. Maybe you'd like to come sometime?"

Time for a Change

"How'd your presentation go?"
"Not well. Remember telling me that if I felt nervous, that I should imagine them all sitting there naked?"
"Yes. Did you?"
"That was a bit too risqué for me, so instead I imagined them sitting in their underwear."
"And?"
"Disgusting. Some of those people should change their underwear more often!"

Incineration Pending

"We completed all the usual tests in this particular planetary environment, beginning with microorganisms."
"Any surprises with microorganisms?"
"None. They reproduced as expected, depleted resources necessary for survival, and, then, in the resulting toxic environment, all died. Afterwards, all remaining experimental material was incinerated."
"Very good. So, as far as microorganisms were concerned, this planetary environment appeared to function as expected."
"Yes. But investigation of the technologically dominant species yielded unexpected results. As resources necessary for survival became depleted, members of the species became more likely to kill not only each other, while competing for resources, but also themselves, individually, and in groups, for reasons unknown."
"Interesting. And at the end of the observation period, the entire planet was incinerated, as per protocol?"
"Actually, no. We've extended the observation period, because it appears that the species in question is itself in the process of planetary incineration."

Overpowering Love

"Has this left you bitter? Angry?"
"Think about it. Whoever did this needs the same things we all need: food, clothing, and somewhere to live. They need love. I want them to have food, clothing, and somewhere to live for years to come. I want them to experience the overpowering love of an attentive cellmate."

I Can See How It Might Happen

My personalized license plate was ready to pick up at the DMV today. I'd paid. I'd waited six weeks. Then they wouldn't give it to me because of some minor error on the application. I'd put a lot of thought into just what I wanted to say: ANTIWAR. Now I was ready to kill.

Writer's Retreat

"Retreats haven't helped... Months at the monastery, the beach, the mountains... nothing. There's been no intensity in my writing since those three best sellers I wrote in prison. I'm going back, death row this time. Yes, these are both loaded. One or two of you will be my ticket in. Any discussion before we start?"

Says Who?

"The red and black speckled granite is beautiful. He would've liked that."
"Great choice. It's our number one seller. And this is the correct spelling of his name?"
"Yes, and those are the correct dates."
"Good. Have you decided on an inscription?"
"Let's use his last words: 'Maybe the pandemic wasn't a hoax.'"

Part Time Optimist

"That's a very pessimistic thing to say."
"It's realistic. Pay attention to the world around you."
"Are you like this all the time?"
"No. I wake up optimistic every single morning. Every night when I go to bed, I wonder why."

MISCELLANEA

Give Credit Where Credit is Due

You must complete both questions to receive
Continuing Education credit for this Ethics seminar.
1. Will you recommend this seminar to your
colleagues?
Absolutely!
2. How will this seminar affect your professional
performance?
It will enable me to choose from various potential
facts and expert opinions to ethically justify
absolutely any possible course of action.

There's More to Life Than Bingo

"Are you doing OK here, Dad? You've been here a
month now."
"Are you kidding? Single 83 year-old guy in a place
like this? Fish in a barrel... Charlene every day
between shuffleboard and supper, Connie every night
after bingo... Listen, thanks for coming, but Lori
stops by every afternoon at one."

Free Agent

"Are you OK? You choked on that sandwich and quit
breathing. We got it out."
"It was weird. All of a sudden, I was on a basketball
court and two guys were taking turns picking people
for their teams. Neither one wanted me."
"Did you know these two guys?"
"God and Satan. Got any whiskey?"

Abbreviation

Salutation. Invitation. Fraternization. Stimulation.
Celebration. Conversation. Intoxication.
Fascination. Infatuation. Affectation. Exhortation.
Disputation. Consternation. Insinuation.
Declaration. Defamation. Denunciation.
Vituperation. Instigation. Perturbation.
Exacerbation. Confrontation. Salivation.
Expectoration. Humiliation. Altercation. Penetration.
Retaliation. Perforation. Evisceration.
Exsanguination. Abomination. Annihilation.
Disorientation. Absquatulation. Examination.
Evaluation. Certification. Investigation.
Authorization. Interrogation. Representation.
Obfuscation. Confabulation. Prevarication.
Illumination. Implication. Accusation. Enumeration.
Publication. Contestation. Invocation. Presentation.
Elucidation. Repudiation. Incrimination. Revelation.
Confirmation. Corroboration. Verification.
Reprobation. Peroration. Summarization.
Recommendation. Deliberation. Adjudication.
Ruination. Resignation. Supplication. Penalization.
Incarceration. Condemnation. Anticipation.
Ministration. Ambulation. Immobilization.
Electrification. Expiration. Auscultation.
Documentation. Containerization. Inhumation.
Notification.

Neurological Consultation

"I've been seeing a charming, demented 78 year-old
female in the hospital every day for a wound
infection. Today she said 'Doctor, you're a very
attractive man. I think I'm falling in love.' Do you
think I should increase her dementia medication?"
"Yes, and you'd better check her visual acuity, too."

Cards for Every Occasion

"Welcome to Cards for Every Occasion. How can I help you?"
"Some friends in their sixties are getting married, and..."
"Oh, that's cute!"
"That's what one of her twenty-something coworkers said. Cute!"
"We're seeing more of that as the population ages."
"Calling them cute seems premature. They're only in their sixties. It's not like they're in their eighties."
"Let's see... Here we are. We have regular, humorous, and religious. Which type would you like?"
"Humorous might best help to them adjust to their new status."
"OK. This section is all humorous premature cuteness cards."

Intangible Benefits of Mime School and Poker

"Dude, look at that hitchhiker. It's late, dark, and really cold. There's nobody around but him and a whole bunch of us."
"I bet that heavy jacket he's wearing is real warm. I want that."
"And he's got a pack on his back. Probably a wallet, too."
"Look at this recycling bin, dude. Bunch of bottles. Let's all grab one and see if maybe he wants to make a donation."
"Dude, he just took one glove off and shoved his hand in his coat pocket. Chill."
"Chill? Dude, I'm freezing. Let's go play video games."

LD 50 Studies

"How've you been? Still doing toxicology? Rat studies?"
"I did lots of rat studies, LD 50 studies, but I've moved on."
"LD 50?"
"Lethal Dose. How much of a toxin is required to kill 50% of a population?"
"So what now?"
"Still LD 50 studies, only now with humans and dollars."

Playing Their Last Card

"They had to move him to ICU, and it looks bad. We should send a card."
"This country should have prepared for the pandemic! We've used our stashed get well and sympathy cards. All we have left is one thank you card."
"Should we send it to the president?"
"Only if we change the verb."

Creative Writing Changed My Life

"This is your bibliography? In chronological order?"
"Yes."
"*Investing After Your First Million*. *Your Next Luxury Automobile*. Impressive! *Intense Short Fiction*? This is yours?"
"Things changed."
"*Dawn Poetry*? *Tips for Buying Used Cars*? *Best West Coast Thrift Shops*? This manuscript is your latest? *Best West Coast Homeless Shelters*?"
"I'd appreciate a small advance. Anything helps."

Succinctly Personal

"Writing tombstones? Name, born, died, dates?
That's writing?"
"Many families prefer something more personally
descriptive than just BORN, DIED and the dates.
That's what I write."
"Like what?"
"FINALLY LET SOMEONE ELSE TALK. DIDN'T
COMPLAIN ABOUT THIS HAIRDO. GAVE UP THE
REMOTE. QUIT SMOKING. SHOULD HAVE ASKED
HIS PHYSICIAN IF VIAGRA WAS RIGHT FOR HIM."

Have Fun!

"Yeah, but... Sorry, I've got to take this call. Hello?"
"Have you got a room available tonight?"
"Who's this?"
"Ellen."
"Sure. We can get you into 109 from 11 til 1. You
were with Larry and Renee last time. They're yours
at 11. Have fun! Bye!"
"What was that?!?!"
"Wrong number, wanting a motel room."

Donna?

"Hello."
"Hi. I'd like to speak with Donna please."
"Donna?"
"Yes, I'm trying to reach Donna. Is she there?"
"Just a minute. Hold on... Honey! Honey! Wake up.
Wake up, Honey! Is your name Donna? Oh... sorry...
Hello? No, there's no Donna here. Wrong number."

First Things First

"Dude, did you hear about Vomitus? He was doing a new piercing, slipped, and drilled through his own skull."

"Way cool! He's got the most outrageous piercings and tattoos. I love the ones with naked Jesus and Satan spanking each other."

"So does Innocence. She posted the video, including ink, before calling 911."

Operators Would Have Been Standing By

"Oh, you're listening to that new radio station."

"Yes, it's refreshing. The mix of music is interesting, the announcers are stimulating, and I enjoy their social and political..."

"BEEEEEEEEEEEEEEEEEEEEEEEEEEEEEEP... This is a test. This is only a test. In the event of an actual emergency, you would have been asked to send a donation."

Can I Put In for a Transfer?

"What's going on? Where am I? How did I get here? Who are you? And what's with the long white robe?"

"Welcome to Heaven."

"Heaven? No way! I'm an atheist. Heaven doesn't even exist. And who in the hell are you supposed to be? God?"

"As a matter of fact..."

"And even if this really is true, there's no way I want to spend all eternity with a bunch of holier-than-thou evangelists!"

"Don't worry. Not many of them end up here."

I Never Told You About Them Before?

"The voices woke me up at about 5 AM. I'd been up late..."
"The voices?"
"Yeah. They were excited, talking fast. I could only make out fragments of sentences. I wrote some of it down, went back to sleep, then rewrote it later. Want to hear this new story?"
"First tell me about these voices."

Thank You So Much

"The rest of us on the committee certainly have tremendous appreciation for your most recent input."
"Thank you. I'm always glad to help in any way possible."
"I'm delighted to hear that."
"Of course."
"I must say that your current recommendation for extensive revision was rather unexpected."
"How so?"
"Even though you've actually attended very few of the biweekly meetings, you've had the opportunity to view the entire process online. You've offered your nonspecific, but enthusiastic, assent from time to time as the project progressed. After ten months of intense work, constant communication, and ongoing revision, the rest of us thought we were done."
"But, after my most recent comments..."
"Precisely why we value your input so much! As you know, the final report is due on Monday. And, this being Friday afternoon, none of us will be disturbing you as you prepare the final report. I'll look forward to reading it Monday morning."

NO! NOT THE SCISSORS!

The Elephant in the Room

"You describe complex situations in very few words. How?"
"Pay attention to what you see, hear, and feel. Find the simplicity in the complexity. Extrapolate the plausible to the ridiculous, the ridiculous to the absurd, the absurd to the obvious. Write it down. Twist, then cut."
"Anything else?"
"Mention the elephant in the room last."

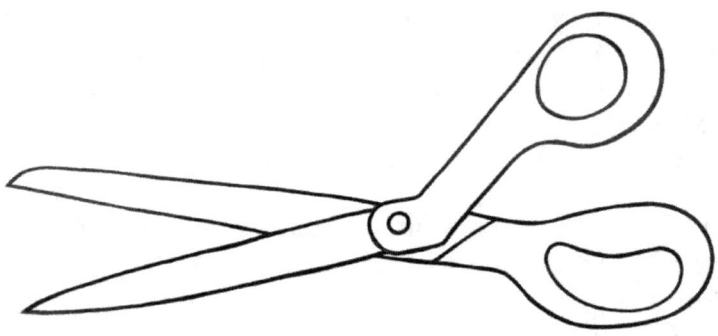

Please Be Kind

"I enjoyed those short stories you just read aloud. Did you write that book?"
"Yes. Thanks."
"I'd like a copy. How much is it?"
"Please be kind, at least try. That's the price of the book."
"You're obviously not expecting it to be a bestseller."
"Think what the world would be like if it were."

But Please Do Try Again Later

"You've read hundreds of your short stories to me over the years, and I love them. You've always written things worth writing, and always done it in an articulate, provocative, entertaining style. For years! And now you're reading me this incoherent blather?"

"But, I didn't…"

"The only good thing I can say about the stories you just read to me is that you can recycle the paper."

"You know that I'm hoping to be published, but I keep getting rejected, and, so…"

"That's no reason to completely change your style and start writing pointless, incomprehensible garbage! You don't even know what those editors want. Stop being such a cheapskate! I'll even split the cost with you. Buy those magazines that keep rejecting your stories, so you can read them and figure out what they're looking for."

"What do you think I've just been reading to you?"

Time to Scribble

I made my living doing something totally different. It did involve some writing, sure, but, at least theoretically, it was nonfiction. At some point, though, I started writing things that I actually admitted were fiction. After enough of that had been published, somebody who was supposed to know about such things said I had a certain "style." Yeah, style, in quotation marks. Only I needed to be even more me, so he said. Unfortunately, the guy was inconsiderate enough to die not long after he said those things. Then somebody else said I sucked. Before long, she dropped dead, too. Anyhow, if you'll excuse me, I'll scribble this down right now. You see, I may be next.

NONBINARY TRUTH

Planning Now for the Future

"Your platform is rather controversial, to say the least."
"Global warming has progressed to the point that our best option for reversing climate change is now a nuclear winter. This will also have the added benefit of eliminating overpopulation. When elected, I will initiate nuclear war immediately. Be sure to vote for me next Tuesday."

Four More Years
(Written the morning after Dubya's re-election.)

Here's a contradance I wrote on November 3, 2004:
Duple Improper
Suggested tunes: Poor Blood for Oil. Let Them
         Breathe Cake.

A1   Circle right.
       Circle right.

A2   Circle right.
       Circle right.

B1   Circle right.
       Circle right.

B2   Circle right.
       Circle right. Face same neighbors.
       Do not progress. Ever.

Note: Some dancers may wish they could sit this one
       out.

Behind the Scenes

"I'll be glad when this election is over."
"Just a few more hours."
"Most people have no idea what goes on behind the scenes. Organizing, coordinating rallies, media coverage, advertising, fundraising, discreet transfer of funds, meetings, deal making, data analysis, social media, and, of course, hacking. But it's not just for our party. It's for the good of our whole country. The people we're electing will do what's best for our country."
"With all this work, did you find time to vote yourself?"
"I love your sense of humor. I voted thousands of times, Comrade."

Living the Dream

"You're having trouble sleeping?"
"I keep having variations on the same disturbing dream every night."
"What's it about?"
"Good and evil. Right and wrong. The world is about to end. Only one person can save it, but it's different people. At the end, they always tell me their names, and that they approve this message."

Look at the Bright Side

"I'm afraid I've got some very bad news for you."
"Just give it to me straight, Doc. What is it?"
"It's cancer, and there's really no good treatment."
"How much time have I got left?"
"Maybe three months."
"Thank God! Now I won't have to lose sleep every night worrying about the election anymore."

WHEN, IF, AND MORE

Don't Hold Your Breath

"What do you want to be when you grow up?"
"An astronaut, and a drummer, and…. Do people keep asking you that? Do they still ask you what you want to be when you grow up?"
"Not for the last fifty years. Now they ask me what I want to be if I grow up."

Bounce

"How was your visit?"
"It was good. We've known each other forever, but we had a lot to catch up on."
"Is she still bouncing from one relationship crisis to another?"
"Always."
"I'm so glad I've got you! And I'm so thankful we don't have that kind of stress in our relationship."
"We don't?"

Oops!

"Daddy! Daddy!"
"Coming… Wow! Jerky! Canned beets! Dried peaches! Keep your radiation suit on. I'll check the counts… It's clean!"
"Why'd they have to have a stupid war?"
"Our president was on the phone with theirs, discussing terrorism. He said 'need new cues' to trigger preventive intervention. The voice recognition system translated 'we'll nuke you.'"

Adjust the Focus

"Going to the game Saturday?"
"No. I'll have relatives that I haven't seen for 20 years visiting next month. I have to do some repairs and cleaning around the house."
"Why? If the place looks too good, they'll be more likely to notice everything that's wrong with you."
"Good point. See you at the game."

In the Stars

"No, I'm an astronomer. I find planets. An astrologer tells you that because of the Moon, Venus, Mars, and Jupiter, you'll propose marriage and hit the lottery. Unfortunately, because of Saturn and Uranus, you'll die suddenly and unexpectedly."
"You won't believe this! Today I proposed and hit the lottery! And... Oh! My chest! It.... I..."

Coffee Plus

"He moved in with you?"
"Yeah. With the pandemic, and isolation, and both of us working from home, I asked him if he would."
"How's that going? It must be sort of like working in an office, having someone else around. I used to work in an office. I always got stuck making the coffee, and got my butt groped for my efforts."
"There has been some of that going on."
"Doesn't that bother you?"
"Not at all! He makes great coffee, and he has a nice butt."

ASSESSMENTS AND PLANS

Just a Temporary Concern

"I'm in high school now."
"Not yet you aren't. You just graduated from junior high. You've still got a couple more months before you're in high school. Be careful, because people your age sometimes do things they later decide were pretty stupid."
"That won't go on forever, will it?"
"No. It's only until you die."

Well Prepared in Some Ways

"Hi. Sorry I'm too late to help."
"That's OK. I got everything set up. I moved the furniture and opened the wine."
"That's a lot of wine. Why so much?"
"I thought..."
"Where's the rest of the food?"
"I thought I should at least taste everything."
"Better open another bottle of wine. I thought you were going to clean the floor. It's filthy!"
"I needed a little nap."
"Better open two more bottles of wine. Then maybe nobody will mind the food or the floor. You did clean the bathroom, right?"
"The bathroom?"
"OK. Open three more bottles of wine, right now. Do you think everyone who's coming over is blind?"
"I think they'll like the play that I wrote so much that nobody will even notice..."
"Right. Better get a bottle of tequila out, too. Someone's at the door. I'll get it."

Have a Nice Day!

"Hey, Doc, answer a question."
"I'm only in this room because my patient's in the other bed. I don't know you."
"You're a good doctor. Look at this. What's the worst thing that could happen?"
"You don't really want my answer."
"Yeah! What?"
"You could die a painful, prolonged, miserable death. Have a nice day!"

Thoughts, Prayers, and Flames

"Another school burning?!"
"Yes, sir. A middle school this time. 17 dead, 22 in burn units."
"We've got to say something! Issue our usual statement saying our thoughts and prayers are with…"
"There's talk again of limiting fuel tank size, sir."
"Excuse me, sir. The president of the National Flamethrower Association is on line 1."

There May Be Other Options

"Hi. How are you?"
"OK, I guess…"
"You don't sound so sure."
"It's occurred to me that I'll probably be in this hospital until I die."
"Have you discussed this with your doctor?"
"I've been a nurse for 48 years. I know what she's going to say: Retire. Then what'll I do with myself?"

Things to Talk About

"Wilkerson, table for one."
"Excuse me, did you drive from Sacramento to
Wisconsin in a VW bug 46 years ago?"
"You were hitchhiking from Reno to Chicago! It can't
get weirder than this!"
"It just did, gentleman. I'll make that a table for
three. Do you remember the redhead in Nebraska
with the flat tire?"

No One Saw This Coming?

"The simultaneous awarding of prizes in Peace,
Medicine, Economics, Chemistry, and Physics to one
individual is unparalleled. But so is the elimination of
overpopulation, hunger, poverty, warfare, global
warming, and numerous diseases. Congratulations,
Doctor!"
"Thanks. My aspirations weren't nearly so lofty when,
as a lonely intern, I developed the first generation
humanoid robotic sexual partner."

Performance Review

"I'd like to start by saying that I've seen and heard
nothing but fantastic things since you've come
aboard."
"I'm a team player."
"Your grasp of, and progress towards, our objectives
is impressive. Our profits reflect this, and so will your
future compensation, including guaranteed book
advances and sales, speaking fees, and
unprecedented campaign funding."

CREATIVE SOLUTIONS

Seeing Is Believing

"We got the whole thing done very reasonably at a wedding chapel up at the lake. Photos of the ceremony, tux, gown, rings... We wanted it all done before her parents came to visit."
"Before?"
"Absolutely. We didn't really want to get married. We told the people at the chapel we were renewing our vows."

Family Reunion

"You've transferred the 10 mill in Bitcoin."
"Yes."
"We've hacked five genetic testing services. Your dad got around. Your best match is a half-brother in Akron. Everything is set. He'll be in Bangkok on the 23rd. You'll get his liver on the 24th. Would you like to meet him first?"
"Of course. He's family."

I Wasn't Prepared for This

"How are you? How're the kids?"
"Everything was fine until they started hanging out with the new kids next door, but now..."
"Oh, no! What is it? Cutting school? Gangs? Drugs? Alcohol? Sex?"
"Those I could deal with, but this... We're now spending every possible moment driving them to practices and games."

The First Step

"Hello."

"Hi. We're Jehovah's..."

"Oh! I'm so sorry! But you've taken the first step. That's so important! Have you tried looking up addiction services? Maybe there's some kind of Anonymous group. Listen, I was just leaving, and... too bad it's not just heroin or meth. Good luck!"

Paperwork Reduction Act

"Put your hands up!"

"That's a very compelling introduction! But, under the circumstances, not a very good idea."

"What? You're a judge on America's Got Robbery? You want me to shoot your ass?"

"That's not a good idea, either, under the circumstances. I definitely advise against that. I suggest that you put the gun away, grab a cup of coffee or soda, on the house, by the way, and leave. No beer, sorry, or I'd have to ask for your ID."

"Give me the money in the register! Now!"

"If you insist. But first, let's think this through. You're not wearing gloves, and you left fingerprints on the door handle when you came in. You could have just pushed the door open with your shoulder, you know?"

"I, uh, hadn't thought about that."

"And you're not wearing any kind of mask. Not even a nylon stocking. Nothing! You know there are security cameras, right? And what about me? Do you know how much paperwork I'll get stuck doing?"

"I, uh..."

"Finally, there are cops who come in here every night for coffee. Some of them pulled into the lot right after you walked in. Again, put the gun away. The cups, coffee, and sodas are right over there."

DIVERSE APPROACHES

Balance

"How do you keep your career and personal life in balance?"
"When disaster strikes in one, it can be balanced by catastrophe in the other. For instance, I got a new boss recently, a real jerk. If he gets any worse, I may have to get married again. Then he won't seem quite so bad."

Gone Fishin'

"How's your Grandpa? I heard he was sick."
"Not anymore. He had a great afternoon. He and Grandma went fishing. They were pulling them out like crazy. Haven't seen him smile so much for years."
"But it's the middle of winter. And she died years ago."
"It's too late to explain that to him."

Comprehensive Lifestyle Planning

"Is your job stressful, your life frustrating, irritation your norm? Do you smile enough? Here at Effitt Lifestyle and Retirement Planners, we know there's more to life, and retirement, than money. A ton of money will do you no good if you let stress and frustration kill you. Need comprehensive planning advice? Just say Effitt!"

If Only

"I thought it might be best to have this conversation with counsel in chambers."
"Agreed."
"Agreed."
"The prosecution charges that the defendant entered the customer service department at Corporation A, and basically commandeered the entire department for several hours. The defense has filed a motion for dismissal, stating that the defendant did so only after months of frustration over unresolved customer service issues. The corporation has filed an amicus brief, stating that while one of its own employees initially called the police at the beginning of the incident, that its position has now evolved. The corporation maintains that the defendant not only got its customer service employees to resolve his own issues, but was also able to get their customer service employees to resolve the problems of a very large number of other customers, and did so very quickly, with impressive customer satisfaction ratings. The corporation suggests that prison time would be inappropriate, and recommends 2,000 hours of customer service."

State-of-the-Art Communication

"Hi. I'm just checking to see who everyone uses for TV, internet, and…"
"How many times do I have to tell you guys not to come back?"
"I'm sorry. We…"
"Just put me on the 'Do Not Bother' list."
"We don't have…"
"Really? You guys are a communications company. Even the Witnesses figured this out."

WELCOME TO THE FUTURE

The Best Things In Life, 2.0

"Professor, as one of the first pioneers to apply nanotechnology to humans, you're one of the few who can really filter the essential concepts from the complexity of these latest developments."
"Thanks. Nanotechnology, combined with the body's own immune system can now target, and manipulate, the molecular switches that control very specific cells within the human body. The technical details are well beyond the scope of this brief interview, but this will soon affect every single one of us."
"Could you please explain the big picture to us?"
"Certainly. Early applications in humans involved the controlled stimulation of new cells within the living, beating heart, radically changing, forever, the treatment of cardiac disease. Major developments have also followed in brain research, with dramatic results for victims of strokes and dementia. This latest breakthrough has now made it possible, for the first time, to accurately measure, and, of course, tax, pleasure."

Galactic Tours Wake-Up Announcement

"During your rest we have approached our next planetary destination. Your appearance now resembles that of the local technologically dominant species. Pertinent linguistic, cultural, and topical information has been transferred. Noteworthy features include espresso, garlic, Cabernet Sauvignon, cheese, jazz, biodiversity, beaches, sunsets, petrochemicals, and ongoing warfare. Remember: Protocol violators will be vaporized. Enjoy your stay."

THIS COULD BE REALLY GOOD!

The Eyes Have It

"You never met her until then?"
"Right. On vacation, camping near a natural hot spring. It's about an hour's walk up a trail in a mountain canyon. I usually have it to myself if I walk in early."
"But this time she's there?"
"We met on the trail on the way up to the spring."
"And you're telling me about her smile, her laugh, her eyes, about water droplets on every lash."
"I never met anyone like her before."
"So, just the two of you, soaking in a remote wilderness hot spring, both completely naked, and what you remember is her eyelashes? Her eyelashes?"
"Yeah. And her email. We're going on our first date next week. I'm excited!"
"You and I are very different. When I'm attracted to a woman, I can't wait to see her with her clothes off. You can't wait to see her with her clothes on."

Parental Guidance

"You'll love this book on wine. Will there be anything else?"
"I've recently learned that I have an adult daughter. None of the books in the 'Parenting' section seemed relevant."
"You may have to write that one yourself. We could discuss this after seven over a glass of Cabernet at the wine shop next door."

Amazingly Lifelike

"Hello."

"Hi. This is Janine, with the Research Department of the Neural Circuitry Division of Lifelike Robotics. Customer Service asked me to call you regarding Unit KD00004."

"That was quick! Thanks for calling."

"Of course. I've had a chance to review the file. KD00004 is..."

"Katie. I call her Katie."

"OK, KD. According to our records, KD has been with you for fourteen months."

"That's correct."

"As a research prototype, KD was provided to you free of charge, and followed very closely for twelve months, as per protocol. All the checkup ratings were 100%. Of course, the team was delighted with that. And all the reports say that you expressed complete satisfaction with all the housekeeping services that KD was programmed to provide, including cooking, laundry, cleaning, and so on. After twelve months, ownership was transferred to you, annual checkups were recommended, and of course, any additional support, as needed. Is all of that correct?"

"Yes, it is, as far as it goes. But there's so much more! She's so lifelike that it's harder every day to remember that she's a robot. And I'd never met anyone like her! She actually listened to me! I couldn't believe how agreeable she was! How compatible we were! This is a little embarrassing, but, I, uh, fell in love with her, and, uh, we, uh, became physically intimate."

"Materials Research will be so excited! How'd it go?"

"It was amazing! And we got married a couple weeks ago."

OR NOT

"Congratulations! You married KD00004! That's so exciting! This has never happened before! I can't wait to share this with the team!"

"But there's more. That's why I called. For the last week, she's been finding fault with everything I do, starting arguments, crying, and screaming. Last night I had to sleep on the couch! I don't know what to do!"

"I see. OK, let's do this. A team of technicians, developers, and I will pick her up at about 5:30 today."

"Thanks! How long do you think your technical evaluation will take?"

"Sir, I don't think you understand. She needs a girls night out."

That Was Then

"What's the matter?"

"I can't get this stupid thing to work!"

"I'm sorry to hear that. How do you feel about that?"

"What do you mean, how do I feel about it?! Can you fix this thing?"

"Are you frustrated? Angry?"

"I'm becoming that way! Are you going to fix this thing, or not?"

"The old me would have. How many totally avoidable arguments did I cause by always trying to fix things, when what you really needed was for me to just listen?"

"The hell with your listening! You fix this thing right now!"

Blindsided

"But you two were lovebirds for years!"
"I thought so. I'm still in shock. We snuggled every single night."
"You didn't see this coming? No warning signs?"
"No arguments, nothing. And now it's over."
"What did she say?"
"She won't even discuss it."
"Who's the other guy?"
"She dumped me for a body pillow."

Sunday Morning

Where am I? Drank too much... My neck feels bruised. There was a guy... his place? Oh!! He's on the floor, bloody, knife in his chest! Fingerprints! Trace evidence! Stay calm. Remember my purse, phone, bra, undies. Look around... No security system. Gloves by the sink. Washing machine, detergent, bleach, rags, bucket, mop... Cleaning day...

Virology Update

"This highly contagious disease has caused immeasurable pain and suffering for millions. Severe cases may lead to anorexia, insomnia, delusions, and even death. We've finally identified the causative virus, and are currently testing a promising vaccine."
"Incredible! Excuse me, Professor. For those who've just tuned in, we're discussing HLV, the Human Love Virus."

THE SANDS OF TIME

Utmost Sincerity

"He'll be missed."
"He was always so thoughtful."
"A wonderful man..."
"A great guy..."
"If only God would bring him back."
"Look! There's a cloud above the coffin!"
"Is that God in the cloud?"
"I've heard your prayers. Dry your tears. I'll bring him back."
"Wait a minute!"
"Hold it!"
"Not so fast!"
"No! Don't!"

This Will Fit into the Schedule

"Sorry to keep you waiting. It's been crazy all day. Mr. Johnson?"
"No, I'm..."
"You're not Johnson?"
"No, I'm..."
"Look, whoever you are, we'll have to reschedule."
"I'm afraid that's not possible. You're on my schedule right now."
"What's this about? Who are you?"
"It's about chest pain. My name's Reaper. Call me Grim."

A Period of Inactivity

"Your palm, the cards, and your astrological chart, with progressions and transits, are all very consistent. I see a period of intense anger and denial, then, soon, a prolonged period of... inactivity. I see a funeral..."
"I'm not going to any funeral!"
"You'll definitely be at this one. I'll need payment in cash today."

Feel the Burn?

"The doctor says it could all be over any time now."
"So I heard."
"Repent now, while there's still time!"
"You know I'm an atheist. Save your breath."
"You could be burning in hell any minute!"
"That would certainly be an effective way to restore my belief in the existence of a loving Heavenly Father."

Factual Massage

"My husband died yesterday. We need an obituary. They tell me you're a writer."
"I've never written an obituary in my life."
"I'll pay you for it. If it's good enough I'll pay a lot."
"You don't understand. I write fiction."
"As you learn about my husband, you'll realize that's exactly what we need: fiction."

Late Breaking News, Christmas Eve Edition

"Police tonight are investigating a series of bizarre home invasions believed to involve a getaway vehicle parked on the roofs of the victims. This just in... The alleged perpetrator, described as an elderly, obese, Caucasian male, wearing red clothing, has reportedly been shot and killed by an armed homeowner. Up next: our exclusive NRA interview."

Saturday, 11:30 AM

"So, fourteen of you came over here, made coffee..."
"He did eleven different roasts this week, Detective. He had coffee parties all the time. He said if this happened, to have the party first, then call. Here, you haven't tried the medium roast Burundi yet."
"Mmmm... excellent... but I've got to call the coroner soon."

But Not the Last

"I wish we'd never even met! You think you're so special! God's gift to women! Always acting like you're the only man on Earth!"
"But, I..."
"We had an amazing place to live! It was Paradise, compared to this dump! Thanks to you!"
"But, I..."
"I told you not to pick that damned apple, Adam!"

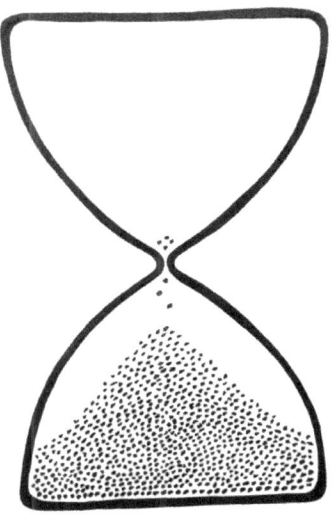

I Can't Take It for One More...

It was a challenge at first. A whole story in 55 words? And the next several were fun. But it became an obsession, with my entire life divided into segments of 55 words. Everything! I can't take it anymore. I don't mean to hurt anyone with this, but I've got to end it right...

PREVIOUS PUBLICATION

Portions of *Verbosity Constrained* have previously appeared elsewhere, either in print or online.

These have appeared in *New Times:*
      "Bathrobe Pending" (2016)
      "A Good Sponsor Is Hard to Find" (2016)
      "The Current State of the Chess Set" (2017)
      "Why Waste Time?" (2017)
      "Utmost Sincerity" (2017)
      "They're Favored This Time" (2017)
      "In the Wool" (2018)
      "A Period of Inactivity" (2018)
      "There's No Place Like Home" (2019)
      "Living the Dream" (2019)
      "Once May Be Enough" (2020)
      "We Do the Best We Can" (2020)
      "How Many?" (2020).

These have appeared in *Reno News & Review:*
      "The Gazette-Journal" (2001)
      "On the Playa" (2019)
      "His Name Is Charlie" (2020).

"Four More Years" appeared in *Country Dance and Song Society News* (2005).

"International Trade" appeared in *El Adelantado de Segovia* (2019) after being translated into Spanish by Nick Webb.

"Yeah, Really" was read and recorded at an open mic session at the National Cowboy Poetry Gathering in Elko, Nevada (2019).

These have appeared in *Ad Hoc Fiction:*
"Thank You So Much" (2018)
"The Eyes Have It" (2018)
"The Eye of the Beholder" (2019)
"A Bit of an Upgrade" (2019)
"Learning the Basics" (2019)
"Vary Charming" (2019)
"And Breathe" (2019)
"Comprehensive Security System" (2019)
"Focus" (2019)
"The Best Things in Life, 2.0" (2019)
"It's a Relative Thing" (2019)
"But Please Do Try Again Later" (2019)
"Tick, Tock" (2019)
"Her Perspective" (2019)
"And Her Perspective" (2019)
"I Scream, You Scream" (2019)
"Healthcare Update" (2019)
"Later That Same Day" (2019).

ACKNOWLEDGEMENTS

This could not have been written without the inspiration provided by quite a few people. Most of them are appreciated. Some family, friends and acquaintances were kind enough to listen as the evolving words were read aloud. Some were even willing to read parts of this aloud to a group. That was especially helpful. Even more helpful were the wine-sipping volunteer proofreaders. There were also some professionals who included portions of this either in their print publications or on their websites.

ABOUT THE AUTHOR

If you've already read all this stuff and looked at all the illustrations, then you already know too much about the author. If you haven't, it doesn't matter.